Shadows Over Augustine

Gabe Straight

To my mom who listens to me ramble, and to my dad who inspires me to ramble.

I

I would've never thought that while being dragged into a car, I would start to think of my father. But if you ever saw Dad's Chrysler, you'd know why. It was the same car my dad took me to baseball games, the same car I drove my prom date in, the car he loved almost as much as he loved me. This car was a darker shade of green than the one I remembered, but in the dead of night, it might as well have been the same. It was in very good shape for its age. Whoever drove this car loved it, just as my old man did. It was all in the details—the sheen along the doors, the polished wooden finish, no dirt or wear to speak of.

But the night chill snapped me out of it. The frigid air whipped against my face as bits of dirt and sand crushed under my feet. I looked out on the lake nearby and could hear the ice-cold waters brush up along the shore through the breeze. My left eye was swollen, and my right eye wasn't doing much better. The sweat and blood streaming down my face both chilled and burned my skin. My five o'clock shadow brushed against my jacket collar like sandpaper. I'd been in plenty of fights, fair and unfair, but I'd never felt the pain I felt that night, physical or mental. And for all I knew, it would be the last thing I ever felt.

Whoever dragged me into that car had fists that could break through stone and huge gold rings that squeezed against my shoulder blades. He pushed me into the back seat, bumping my head on the way down. The blood that was fisted out of me dripped on the seats, looking like soda stains. Staggering, squirming, struggling, I made my way to the window and sat myself up.

I'd seen Augustine from this angle dozens of times taking the train, and it was as beautiful as it ever was. Even from here, I could see the tiny lit windows in the skyscrapers just below the clouds, the cars seemingly chasing their own headlights as they wind down the maze of streets. I thought to myself as I stared out, *Lord knows if I'll ever see any of this city again.*

So what sort of nonsense led me here, barely alive in some Chrysler next to a beach, knocking on death's door?

It all started with the car.

Growing up, I had a hard time staying out of trouble. I ran with a group of punks that stole auto parts. We were efficient; in the dead of night, we could nick a car radio in five minutes flat. We were regulars at the junkyard and antique store. There were no cars off limits, no place we wouldn't go to, no part we couldn't steal if we wanted to.

My dad taught me everything I needed to know about cars from the Chrysler he kept in his garage. I watched him take care of it and fix it time and time again. Sometimes, he'd grab me and take me out on the road—nowhere in particular, just out of the house so he could take a drive. That thing meant the world to him and showed me every day just how much it did.

One day, the boys were talking to me about a sweet score they were checking out in a nicer part of town. When they described the car, I realized they were talking about the same exact same car as the one my dad had, the Chrysler. And just like that, all the cars I worked on stopped belonging to no one. They belonged to people, people who needed them and loved them and cared for them just like my dad did. The harm we were doing to people struck home like it never had. After that moment, I couldn't steal from cars anymore.

The rest of that week was a blur. I remember telling my friends that I couldn't join them on a heist because I had something else planned, and then I sent in a tip to the cops so they'd all get busted. I was really conflicted about all of it for quite a while, but then, one night, I told my dad everything. After I told him, I remember he walked over to me in the kitchen, put his arm around me to let me know there was nothing I could do to make him love me any less, looked me in the eye, and said, "When no one's around to do the right thing, then it's up to you to do the right thing."

And just like that, I was a new man. I had my mantra, my way of life, and I figured it was about time I put it to good use.

Five or so years later, I completed basic training at the Rutherford Police Academy, which is about half an hour south of my hometown. They gave me my first patrol as an officer. I had some growing pains, but in due time, I could pick apart a crime scene as well as anybody. I learned all the ways someone could lie to me, and I helped out plenty of good people. It took some time, but eventually, people started to like me, and I felt like I was making a real difference. I even adopted Midnight, my three-year-old black Siamese who's even sweeter than she looks.

I wish that was the whole story, but it goes on to have plenty of corruption and lies. It's a story about a commissioner who took too many bribes from the banks, banks that had too many mob ties, and me, a cop who couldn't take any more of it.

It all left a bitter taste in my mouth, made all the worse by having to wear the same uniform as the cops who knew everything that was happening and did nothing about it. So, one day, I threw my badge on the commissioner's table, grabbed my things, and made my way to Augustine in hopes of starting a new life as a private investigator.

Augustine was another town nearby, farther out east. Working on my own, I didn't need to worry about dirty cops and shady deals on my way to do some real good. I was really starting to think I could do some good work in Augustine. Unfortunately, that wasn't the case.

It didn't take me long to figure out that, in Augustine, you couldn't walk down the street past sundown and come home with all your money and no bruises. Your house was broken into once a week or so, and if you owned a business, you had to slip some money to the mob to keep your bones unbroken (well, mostly unbroken). Crime was everywhere. Neighbors stole from neighbors, and local stores sold baseball bats, but nobody played baseball. Nobody had anything nice, and if you weren't brushing up with the rich banker types or their high-end lawyers, you couldn't afford anything nice anyway. There were some alleyways people would walk blocks out of their way to avoid, and they still do. I can't say I blame them.

Mayor Church kept saying he would try to fix Augustine, but he mostly just banged his head against the wall. Word would get out about failed sting operations and stakeouts that went nowhere, which just reinforced the common belief that the mobs were unstoppable.

But one family gave Church and the rest of Augustine far and away the most headaches: the Salentinos.

The Salentino family made money better than anyone. They were a part of everything: the docks, the vending machines, private security, construction, the laundromats. If you made money doing something in Augustine, so did the Salentinos. They operated exclusively in Augustine, but even I knew about them back in Rutherford. Families like the Ciccilinos and the D'Vellos were basically hired guns for the Salentinos, and everyone knew it.

At the top stood Catalina Salentino, otherwise known as "The Tiger" to those who feared her, which was pretty much everyone. She was formidable, six and a half feet and two-hundred-fifty pounds of pure muscle, a mastermind who was suave enough to sell snow to Eskimos and then beat them to within an inch of their lives if they didn't pay up. After a handful of failed assassination attempts, legend started that she had bulletproof skin.

Needless to say, most of my work in Augustine consisted of people coming to me with problems caused by the Salentinos. Some days, I would look outside my office to find a line going down the hall and out the door. Dozens of weary and frightened people came to the only person in the city who might be able to help them. The cops were too busy with the mob itself to worry about the people they were stealing money from.

Goddammit, I wanted to help. I wanted to solve every murder, get all the lost money, and find every mother's missing son. But you never know just how many people need your help, how many heartbreaking stories lead to nowhere but dead ends, and how much later your bedside alarm clock says it is every night as you lay down to sleep. There were more people in line every day, and the cases became nearly impossible to solve.

My gut started to tell me something. It was a whisper at the back of my head that I'd been happy to push down on many times before. But this time, it was different; it knew it was right. Every day, that feeling in my gut got more intense, and by the time I took a moment to notice it, it was all I could think about. I couldn't ignore it anymore.

I gave up. It was the hardest thing I ever had to do in my life, without question. I didn't drop any gigs (I'm not that much of a monster), but I stopped taking new cases. I couldn't look myself in the mirror for weeks after that.

I knew folks wouldn't take the news well, but that doesn't mean I was prepared for it. I had plenty of screaming faces outside my door, even a couple rocks thrown through the glass. It wasn't the screaming or the rocks that hurt the most; it was the looks they gave me when they were done yelling when they truly accepted that they'd never know what happened to their missing kid or know who killed their wife. I think about those looks every day. It took a lot of strength to try and help them all, but even more strength to tell them I couldn't.

The open cases dwindled as the weeks went by until there wasn't any line outside my door to speak of.

I wish I could tell you I eventually got numb to it. But the pain never goes away. It only swells until it's all I can think about most of the time. I still see blood stains in parts of the city, the scars that hide the good person whose blood it was, and all the good people who I knew had shed blood somewhere in the city, dripping down some sewer drain.

For the next month and a half, this former PI with a difficult relationship with God prayed on his bedside for his former clients and everyone in the city to get what they deserved, and for a city that only knew crime and chaos to give itself a break.

And just when we didn't think Augustine had any chance, Mayor Church came through with nothing short of a miracle. You should've seen his face as he was walking to the podium for that press conference, grinning from ear to ear and practically skipping up the steps. It was pure pandemonium. Church and the police force had finally managed to get dirt on Tiger and the entire Salentino family in one sting, courtesy of a box full of every name and under-the-table check they ever wrote thrown into a dump just outside of town.

It took only a couple months to throw them all in prison, where they'd never again see the light of day. Once the main Salentino family was out of the picture, their musclemen, movers, and suppliers were never heard from again. For the first time anyone could remember, the blood stopped dripping down the drain, the deli windows stayed unbroken for more than a week, and trash cans down all the alleys stopped burning. We marveled at the lack of broken bones and fell comfortably into this new way of living.

Of course, Mayor Church was lauded as a hero. His determination to stop the Salentinos made him the most liked person in Augustine, and it wasn't even close. His approval rate shot up so high no one would even entertain the thought of someone else being in charge of Augustine. It doesn't mean the mobs were done for good. We still had a couple other families making a bit of trouble in certain parts of the city. But compared to the Salentinos, they were no bigger concern than any other small-time criminal the cops dealt with.

With the Salentinos gone, I knew Augustine was turning over a new leaf. I could see the faces of people on the street, as much relief as could be. The sun shone brighter after that; hell, I saw flowers bloom for the first time in God knows when.

With my reputation as a private eye in the toilet, I had to start looking for other work. Most places I looked at didn't have any use for me. Some of the places knew who I was and knew better than to hire me. Eventually, I had to settle on a part-time gig working in a factory. I wasn't making nearly as much money as the other job, but it was something, and I was able to make sure Midnight and I had our favorite meals from time to time: tuna with bits of celery and carrot and corned beef on marble with horseradish and plenty of mustard, respectively.

But even after the sighs of relief and calm nights alone that ended with an early night's sleep, something didn't sit right with me. My gut was talking again, followed by a thought that burrowed into my head with no intention of getting out any time soon... how much longer could this truly last? The Salentinos were gone, but I began to think that it was only a matter of time before it happened again, before another syndicate filled the void the Salentinos left behind, a family that would be smart enough to not leave silver bullets at the bottom of a dump.

Nothing this good stays that way forever, not in a city that has been defined by chaos and dirty men for so long. I got more concerned each night as I looked out my window, afraid of how many people were on the brink of losing their loved ones all over again. Was it already here? That was the most frightening idea. *No*, I thought to myself. I would know once it came. At least, I hoped I would.

II

It was October. Long gone were the humid mornings of September when you could leave your window open to let in the fresh air. We now had to deal with the morning frost blanketing the early hours with an icy chill.

My day started just like any day. I rose at 6:30 to an inkling of sunshine peeking through the bottom of my window. Midnight hopped up onto my bed and rubbed against my ankle, making sure I didn't forget her breakfast. Luckily, today was Saturday, the start of my weekend, so I decided to celebrate. Compared to the day-old chicken parm in my fridge, Marco's was definitely the better breakfast idea. Once Midnight was taken care of, I left my apartment and headed north.

Along the way, I walked past Mayor Church's campaign office. It was a bit odd seeing a campaign office for someone with no risk of getting voted out, but sure enough, there it was. The office was between the laundromat and another office building, covered in tomato-red posters plastered with Church's face, buttons, flags, stickers, the works. On one of the posters plastered along the window was Church's winning and warm smile. However, it was just a bit unsettling as his eyes seemed to be staring right at me. One of the volunteers perched outside in a lawn chair stood up and approached me as I passed.

"Can Mister Church count on your vote this election?" She held it in her hand like a peace offering. I took it and put it in my pocket.

"Why even think of having a different mayor?" I happily replied.

I looked her in the eye, and once I knew who it was, I almost regretted leaving my apartment. It was Deborah Weaver, the mother of a kid who got into too much trouble with the mob. She was the first case I had to turn down, leaving her nobody to find her son. She had heard about my reputation, and she knew that if anyone in the city had a chance to find her son, it was me. That day, she was the first person in line, ready to set herself on the path to seeing her son again, and I had to block it off. The thousand-yard stare she sent right into my soul haunts me to this day.

And here she was, all that time later. Her warm and friendly look crumbled into a grimace when she recognized me.

"Six hundred forty-nine days, Mister Reeves. Just because you won't look for him doesn't mean my son isn't out there."

"I know, Ms. Weaver," I lamented.

It looked like she was waiting for me to say something. I bit my lip, stepped to her side, and began to distance myself from her.

"I bet you don't even remember his name," she crowed. I turned my shoulder back at her, that same expression on her face.

"His name is Jeremy, and I'm still sorry for everything," I said back.

I never forget a name, even if I want to forget why I know it. It was quick, but I could see a slight change of expression on her face. Her eyes started to loosen up, and her pursed upper lip drooped and relaxed ever so slightly. Maybe she knew I felt awful about giving up on her like I did everyone else. But with a slight shake of the head, she snapped herself out of it. I dropped my gaze and trudged on ahead.

Luckily, Marco's was just down the street, and it was both the best celebratory breakfast and emotional uplift I could ever ask for. Marco's Premiere Delicatessen had been open as long as anyone could remember, and it was the unofficial best place to eat in the whole city. Marco Roselli himself still manned the front and was just about the friendliest person anyone had ever met. He knew every customer by name, mostly because they all came to his shop three times a week. He knew everyone's orders, and if he saw you heading in, he could sometimes have your turkey club ready for you by the time you said "Hello." Sure, the place got hit here and there like everyone else, but he always had the money to fix it. Once you take a bite of his Italian roll, there's no going back.

And, of course, it was plenty busy around breakfast time. Only a few tables and chairs were empty. The place was as warm as ever, though a bit greasy. Customers perched atop the squeaky stools along the counter while their conversations filled every corner. I'm pretty sure I and the rest of Augustine could draw the place from memory; it was practically a second home.

Marco saw me walk in and smiled a wide, toothy grin.

"The usual, Danny?" he asked.

"Too easy, we'll do lox on wheat, no onion," I responded.

He didn't hesitate. "Daring today, aren't we? Well, your little unusual for the day is an extra three bucks."

I dug through my pockets for his $7.39 and placed it on the counter. The money and my lox were like passing ships in the night.

The other thing I liked about Marco was that he saw the good in everyone. He knew from the gossip everything he could know about me, but he also understood where I was coming from. Sometimes, you just gotta know when to quit, as he said to me. Marco was one of the few people in Augustine who knew my reputation and still didn't completely hate me.

A bell from behind me let me know another regular came in. I stepped to the side, and Marco tipped his cap.

"Hey Tony, sorry to hear about your brother," Marco said.

Tony, a skinny guy with a sizable protruding nose, looked up and nodded solemnly.

"Thanks, Marco. The usual?" Marco was already wrapping up Tony's salami sub by the time he walked up. As Tony reached out with his change, I noticed his inner pocket kept a rather nice-looking silver flask with a gem in the center. He dropped his change on the counter, grabbed his sub, and walked out with barely a sound.

"Shame what happened," Marco said. "Brother was an honest working man, hit his head on the coffee table just last night, out cold, then bled himself to death."

"His brother?" I said.

"Paulie Fisher, yeah. Worked at the car shop down the street, took a turkey on rye."

"Yeah, sounds awful," I said.

"Yeah, he was a good kid... good kid," Marco mused.

He looked around at the other customers to see if anyone was close by and then leaned into me.

"I don't like it, Danny. Paulie was a bit of a space cadet, but he wasn't no klutz," Marco said. "You didn't hear this from me, but Paulie was supposed to get a big check from the shop. Insurance for a busted leg."

"A busted leg? No wonder he tripped," I said.

"But that's the thing," Marco said. "The check was fat, four or five figures. Cashed the check, and then a couple hours later, he's dead. Don't that sound off to you?" I knew what he was getting at.

"I'm sure the police will tie those loose ends together without me looking over their shoulders," I said.

"Cops already ruled his death an accident. Shut the case before even opening it."

"I'm not putting the hat back on for a bad look," I said bluntly.

"I know, you hung it up. All I'm saying is, it don't sit right," he said.

"Not my job to worry about that anymore," I replied. Marco sighed.

"You don't need to be a private eye to know Paulie didn't trip, and you know it whether you want to or not."

Marco could probably tell I still had my doubts.

"Fine, Danny, you got me. I'm asking for a favor. Paulie was one of my favorite regulars, and I wanna know what, or who, got to him. Here."

Marco grabbed my receipt off the table and scribbled an address with a pen. As he did, another ring, another customer.

Marco looked into my eyes. I didn't need to say anything for him to know I was thinking about it. Maybe it was just an unlucky day for Paulie, but if it wasn't? I got why Marco thought there was more to this. These were not just coincidences. If Marco had all his facts straight, this might be something worth looking into. But what if he was wrong? After everything I went through the last time I was a PI? One more drop down the wrong rabbit hole, and Midnight and I would have to skip town for good. The last thing I needed was another one of those on my conscience.

Nothing in the world could've taken my eyes off that receipt. It's just a piece of paper, but that address made it feel a million pounds heavier. I grabbed my lox, put the address in my pocket, and headed out the door. Marco nodded as I left.

To be honest, the biggest reason I grabbed the receipt initially was to get Marco's eyes off me. Marco was known for crazy stories that were anything but straight from the horse's mouth, so maybe he got something wrong. Maybe he loved Paulie so much he assumed the worst about his death. Maybe Paulie Fisher really did hit his head on the coffee table, and that was all there was to it.

The address Marco scribbled on the receipt was on the other side of the block where I lived. Naturally, it was separated by a fork in the road because this kind of decision couldn't have been made easy for me. I made my way to the fork as the sun set over the harbor and rested barely above the ocean edge. The clouds radiated a stunning magenta and orange across the entire sky. To the left of the street was another calm night alone with Midnight, where I'm supposed to be, where I don't make any more trouble. To the right of the street was Paulie Fisher's body, still warm on his apartment floor. Paulie Fisher's death was probably an accident, and Marco probably got some details wrong.

I crumpled up Marco's receipt, threw it on the ground, and began to head home.

Digging my hands into my coat pockets, I felt something poke at the tip of my finger. I took out the campaign pin Mrs. Weaver gave me, as shiny and tomato red as ever. I held it, and it became an anvil in my palm.

Jeremy Weaver was this wide-eyed deer of a kid who thought working for a mob-owned bar was a good idea. Way back when, his mother told me Jeremy decided one night he'd had it with the low pay and long hours, so as he put it, he "took a bit off the top." He walked to work the next day the same as always, but after that, he was never seen again. No one thought Jeremy Weaver going missing was suspicious either, or rather, no one cared enough to think it even was suspicious. I clenched the button in my palm, turned, and headed to the right. Six hundred forty-nine days.

III

The apartments in Augustine were mostly built by the same contractor, so they bore very similar traits. I made my way to Paulie Fisher's place, and if not for the remnants of a number on the wall, I would never have found it. All six stories featured missing bricks and boarded-up windows.

I entered the lobby to be greeted by the peeling wallpaper and a hungover employee at the desk. *Don't mind if I do.* I inspected the mailboxes in the lobby and found "Fisher" under room 5D. As much as I couldn't trust the stairs, given the state of the rest of the building, I sure as hell couldn't trust the elevator. As I suspected, the stairs that weren't broken in half creaked with every step.

Five stories and some empty breaths later, I found myself in a dusty hallway. The numbers on all the doors were either worn out or gone entirely. Luckily, I could see a couple cops loitering outside a door covered in yellow tape. The cops mentioned something about a glass of water and headed down the other side of the floor. I pushed the police tape aside to make a hole for me and entered the room.

Unlike the rest of the building, Paulie Fisher's room was as clean as a whistle. Two glass windows framed a beautiful skyline view of Augustine. I got down and pinched the floor for dust. Someone sweeps up here often. Whether that was Paulie Fisher or another detective was to be determined.

The man of the hour lay face down above a shallow pool of blood by the coffee table. He wore a yellow sweater over a button-down shirt and khakis with a huge cast covering his left leg.

A fireplace rested in the corner, long burned out. On the other side, a kitchen island housed two chairs and two dinner placemats. *That must be for his brother Tony.* I decided to see what I could find in the bathroom. In the medicine cabinet, an assortment of cold and flu pills and nothing else. The shower didn't reveal any immediate clues; it was clean as a whistle, just like the rest of the place.

My best chance now to find some secrets would be the bedroom, so I made my way there. There was just a single dresser resting parallel to the bedroom door. I rummaged through the drawers to find just the usual shirts, pants, socks, and underwear that anyone would have. The closet didn't house very many skeletons either, more of the same from the drawer.

I began to close the closet when something caught my eye: there was a suit jacket inside a very large plastic cover from the cleaners. The jacket was clearly too big to fit Paulie. I pulled the clothes hanger toward me to inspect it. I felt around the jacket for something in the pockets, and sure enough, I felt something sewn into the fabric of the jacket. I took my knife out to cut it open and found a manilla folder.

There was nothing in the folder, but the tab of the folder had a symbol drawn onto it: a black dot inside of a circle. But that didn't tell me anything useful. The body would have more answers.

I crept up to Paulie's head and gingerly held it up. There was a noticeably large gash on his forehead, with blood tracing itself back to the source. I checked the coffee table, and sure enough, a splotch of blood rested on the corner. I looked around his feet for something he could trip on but found nothing out of the ordinary.

Behind Paulie was an armchair. It was clean but not without its tears and bruises, befitting a chair that had been well-used. Could Paulie have tripped on one of the chair's legs? I think the rest of the apartment would've told me if Paulie kept anything out of line. An ordinary, unlucky fellow might have tripped, but his apartment was telling me that Paulie was not an ordinary fellow.

I checked to see if the armchair had been moved. The rug was a light color, so any dragging would be easily recognizable. There wasn't any. I lowered myself to the floor to check the armchair legs and underside. Under the chair, the apartment threw me a bone: a hardcover book lay open with the pages down. So the armchair hadn't moved since before Paulie died. It was time to get in the mind of Paulie Fisher.

But first, I wanted to see if the armchair could have caused his death. I got up and made a beeline to the kitchen, prepared myself like a runway model, and then briskly walked to the armchair. I made sure to go out of my way and hit the legs of the chair. Carefully, I dropped myself to the ground, but my head landed almost three feet away from the coffee table. There was no way the armchair was the culprit.

I checked around the vicinity for anything else that could've made Paulie trip, but there was nothing of the sort. Paulie couldn't have tripped to his death, which meant that I couldn't rule out foul play from another party. I had to give the house one more look around. The devil's in the details, so all I had to do was put my eyes on the right one.

It had to wait, however, as I was interrupted by a noise from outside the apartment. It sounded like the cops were back, and they wanted to have a look at Paulie, too. I dashed into the closet and closed the door. Through the crack, I saw two cops stroll into the apartment. One had blond hair and a face ripe with acne. The other had brown hair and a noticeable gut.

"See, look, I told you. He tripped. Can I go home now?" the blond one said.

"Well damn, I guess you're right. But what about the insurance money he was going to collect? That's kinda odd."

"What about it? Bloody gash on his forehead, blood splattered on the table, case closed. He just had a bad day, that's all."

The brown-haired cop scanned the room. Seeing the way his head turned, I could tell he didn't have a knack for forensics. Nevertheless, he made his way into the bedroom just like I had done moments before. "Clean as a whistle, let's just go." The blond cop sneered.

This was clearly the wrong time to bump my head on the door. It wasn't a bang, but it was enough to get the blond cop's attention. I tensed up and felt around for anything I could hide behind. The cop strolled to the closet and opened the door, but all he saw was a couple boxes and the winter jackets I hid myself behind. I was squished against the closet wall, sucking my stomach in hard. I didn't know how much longer I could keep it that way.

"You know if the bakery up the street is still open?" the brown-haired cop called out from the bedroom. That was enough for the blond cop to give up on his closet search.

"Yeah, the one on Storrow Drive? They close at eight, we better run." The sounds of footsteps and a door slam let me know it was safe to leave.

Now, where was I? Ah, yes, the devil in the details. I wiped the sweat off my forehead and traversed the apartment again. Hopefully, I could catch something the cops before me couldn't. Judging by the last two, the odds were looking good. What was left? The kitchen had nothing, and the same was true for the bathroom. The bedroom opened the door for secrets but didn't confirm a killer. The family room only showed Paulie didn't trip.

I looked over at the front door. Everything Paulie would take with him outside was on it: a hanger for his coat and hat and a smaller hanger for a wallet and keys. He clearly had a system in place to keep everything in order, as was consistent with the rest of the apartment. But I still had more questions than answers. I had to look harder.

I looked out at Paulie's view for a moment. Behind a chair and ashtray stand was a glass window so clean you couldn't even see it... and a peculiar-looking rug.

It didn't really look like a rug. I walked up to it and felt it. It was too light. There was no dust, no dirt, not even a scratch. The rug was too clean to be what Paulie walked on before he had his smoke overlooking the city.

I lifted it up, and all my questions started to look a lot clearer: footprints. On top of that, this "rug" shared the same color scheme as the couch. It had to be a throw blanket. Maybe there wasn't a perfect case for murder, but there sure as hell was one for foul play. There was only one person I could think of now who could help me, and that was Tony Fisher.

IV

The next morning, I headed to Tony's apartment, in a building a couple blocks away from Paulie's. Marco said they were as close as siblings could be. The only person who knew Paulie better than himself was Tony, and that was what I was hoping for. I got off the elevator, made my way to Tony's apartment, and knocked on the door.

"Mister Fisher? Mister Fisher," I called. I heard creaking footsteps before Tony revealed himself, peeking out from behind the door.

"Yes? Are you from the paper?" Tony peeped.

"I am not. My name is Danny Reeves, I'm a private investigator. Can I ask you some questions?" Tony began to shrink away from the door but then looked me in the face.

"You're the guy from Marco's the other day," Tony says.

"I am. Hell of a pastrami, huh?" I said, trying to lighten the mood.

Tony nodded and stopped white-knuckling the door. He motioned for me to come in. The apartment was a little less organized than Paulie's but far from a pigsty.

"Thank you, Tony," I said. "I'm sorry about your loss."

"Thanks," Tony said, slumping into his sofa.

"So, is it true Paulie was about to get an insurance check in the mail?" Tony nodded.

"Car fell on him from above after the jack broke; darn near ripped his leg off."

"Sounds like a pretty heavy check. Was it not?"

"Well, he had to be on crutches and couldn't work, so it was enough to help him along for a month or two."

"How many people knew about this check?" I asked. Tony thought to himself.

"Not that many, I guess. Other than me, people at work probably knew about it. Why do you ask?"

As he answered, my wandering eyes stopped on a desk lamp shining on more than a handful of letters covered in red ink. Tony noticed where I was looking and didn't seem that happy about it.

"Did Paulie make any enemies who would want to take that check away from him?" I asked. Tony wasn't expecting that question.

"Why would you ask something like that? The cops told me he just tripped."

"I'm pretty sure he did." I said, "But I'm just covering all my tracks. It's a bit strange that someone got a big check and died before cashing it, don't you think? Anyone who knew how much money he was getting would want it for themselves."

"I mean, I see where you're coming from, but nobody he knew would kill him for it." Tony finally said after a pause.

"So he had an enemy or two?" I asked. Tony looked around his living room, then out the window.

"That's not what I..." Tony's eyes started to wander. He contorted his lips, readying himself to phrase his words very carefully.

"He never went into much detail about it, but he mentioned sometimes he liked to go to the tracks and spend a bit. That's all he told me."

"Interesting. Maybe he made a bad bet," I thought out loud.

"Again, he barely talked about it," Tony said. "I just remember him saying he'd meet up with his friends down at The Whisper and head to the tracks from there."

Everyone in town knew about The Whisper, but few people had been inside it. It had a reputation for being very lavish and very exclusive. You had to have a pretty penny just to get a foot in the door, much less spend the night. Not many regular people knew what went on in there, and the people who did know weren't going to run their mouths about it. But, if the goons that had something to do with

Paulie's death were hanging out at The Whisper, then that was going to be my next destination. I thanked Tony for his time and headed off.

The Whisper sat comfortably in the center of the town square, between the Callaghan Theater and the State House across the street, making easy access for the rich and powerful. The shining lights flooding from inside The Whisper made everything around it much darker than it was, a beacon of comfort for those with enough money to stay happy.

After sunset, the rain came in like a steady blanket, making puddles that splattered everywhere you went. The wind made everything even wetter than it already was. I was plenty wet by the time my second foot left the taxi.

I made my way across the street and headed to the entrance. Standing firmly at the entrance was a tall, thick, balding man. He wore a three-piece suit that had to have been custom-made. I felt that this guy could probably break me in half with his fingers, so fighting to get through him was not an option.

"I don't know you," the guard grunted once he saw me, unmoving.

"I don't know you either. What are the drink specials tonight?" I asked.

"Nobody gets in that I don't know"—he nudged his bowling ball of a head toward the inside—"or they don't know."

"Well, that's where you're wrong. I got a friend in there waiting for me."

"No, you don't, now beat it." He revealed the brass knuckles in his massive right hand and cracked his neck.

This was not the first place I'd had to break into in my career, not even the first one that week. So, I had some tricks up my sleeve.

I pretended to be defeated and trudged down the sidewalk. After a few steps, I looked down the alleyway next to The Whisper, and... bingo, there was a back door. I worked my way around the block and into the alleyway where that guard couldn't see me, then up to the back door.

Even though I was technically retired, I still kept a bobby pin in my jacket in case of times like this. Lock-picking was never a problem for me. I'd gotten through plenty of doors in my time. But, of course, things weren't supposed to be easy for me today. The rain and wind made my bobby pin slip out of my hands, which were getting progressively more numb. I checked my jacket for more bobby pins, but I only had one, so I couldn't afford to break it; I had to be careful.

It took everything I had, but I did it. I could feel the door slowly unlocking when suddenly I felt the doorknob turning from the other side. I panicked and ducked behind a dumpster as the door opened. A busboy hurled a bag of trash into the dumpster across from me and then went back inside. I grabbed the door just as it began to close completely. I slid it open and made my way inside.

I'd always wondered what heaven would be like, and The Whisper looked like a pretty good answer. Everywhere I looked, I saw gold: the floor tiles, glasses, tablecloths, bowties, curtains, chairs, right down to the trashcans. Everything was either colored gold or had real gold somewhere on it. The ceiling was at least fifteen feet high, with protruding marble columns along the walls. On the other side of where I came in was a sizable sound stage, filled almost completely by a house band banging out a lively, upbeat track. Every seat in the venue circled around a dance floor bigger than my entire studio apartment. Most of the right side was taken up by the bar, where gents in vests with golden bow ties made drinks mixed from unlabeled golden bottles of different shapes and sizes. It was plenty busy, filled with folks wearing the nicest-looking suits and gowns money could buy.

It took me a second to get over all the glamour, but I had to try and fit in long enough to get what I needed. I wasn't exactly dressed to the nines, my dark brown slacks with a button-down shirt and tie. Someone was eventually gonna find out I didn't fit in here.

I sat down at the bar, which was (of course) laced with gold and cushioned arm rests, and ordered a gin rickey. I pretended I was cracking my neck so I could scope out the place without looking suspicious.

Through all the sea of faces, I started to worry. *What the hell was I thinking? Who will talk to me here?* God only knows what some of these people would do once they knew I wasn't supposed to be here, as I thought about my friend at the entrance. I started to feel eyes at the back of my head.

Just then, the band faded into a slower ballad as the lights dimmed. That calmed my nerves a bit—at least, it made it harder to pick me out. The entire room turned its attention to the front of the stage. The hums of conversation almost completely died down as a trumpet played the opening notes. And then *she* walked out.

To say she was gorgeous almost felt like an insult; she was *beyond* gorgeous. She had silky smooth jet-black hair, piercing green eyes accentuated by a golden eye shadow and a sparkling sleeveless gold dress that wrapped divinely around her body. She walked with the confidence of someone who owned the place. I couldn't believe any one person could be so beautiful. As the rest of the band joined in, she crooned about a lost love with a commanding alto. Every note, every run, she sang so gracefully but so passionately at the same time. Nobody in the audience dared to make a sound. With a voice like that, not to mention the way she looked, she could play any stage in the country, on the planet, I was thinking to myself. *What's she doing in a city like this? Singing and rubbing elbows with this type?*

And then it hit me: even if she didn't know every tycoon that came up to her, she must certainly be around them a lot. Maybe one of them bragged a bit too much about their gigs. I could imagine a fellow doing anything to impress someone who looked like her. She was as good a lead as I had, and I had to hurry because the last thing I wanted to do was give my fellow admirers more time to figure out that I didn't belong there.

She finished her song, and the crowd went nuts, going from complete silence to thunderous roars of applause. Roses rained down the edge of the stage until there was a pile of them up to her ankles. It was so loud in there, I didn't think I was gonna be able to pick up her name, but somehow, I was able to hear a common name among the crowd... and that name was Desiree Drake.

The applause grew louder, and Miss Drake came front and center to claim her roses. As if on signal, every fella with working ears and a pulse pushed his way to the stage, reaching out his hands for her to shake while trying to get a compliment or two in.

As much as I also wanted to get close to her (for professional reasons), I knew I had no chance of getting any answers in that mess of a crowd. I had to think a couple steps ahead. I could tell by her body language she was trying to make her way to a door off to the side of the stage. That would provide as good a chance of getting a private conversation as any.

There was enough commotion for me to sneak into the stage door without anyone noticing, or so I hoped. I eked the door open and slipped in. I was in a small hallway with several doors on each side. At the end was another hallway perpendicular to this one. Compared to the room I was just in, this hallway was like a completely different building, with its gray peeling walls and dull wooden doors.

The doors had numbers but no names. Most of the door numbers were silver, but one door all the way down to the left had a number colored gold. As I got closer, I could see pieces of paper jammed into the door's creeks. This had to be it. I grabbed one of the papers. It was a letter addressed to Desiree Drake. Sure, I'd been in love before, but I never imagined sending a love letter to somebody with so many public admirers.

"You can leave the note at the door, and I'll get to it later," a voice said behind me.

I turned around to find Desiree Drake giving me a tired look. She was even more beautiful up close, if that was even possible. My heart was racing just looking her in the eye. Even close up, she had no flaws to speak of. She almost didn't look real.

"Oh no, you got the wrong idea," I said in a bit of a panic. "I didn't write..."

"Thanks, but I've had a long day, and I'm not in the mood to chat, so you can just leave it and go," Miss Drake said.

"I'm not here to give you a letter. I need to talk to you about a case I've been working on. I'm a detective." She stared at me with a look that was both concerned and annoyed.

"Since when does Bruce let private eyes in?" I could see the gears turning in her head. Then, before I could blink, she unsheathed a knife from a thigh holster and pinned me against the wall.

"How about you tell me who you really are unless you want to be dropped to the bottom of a river. Your choice."

"I'm telling the truth, I promise. A man was murdered last night. Word is he was in trouble with some guys who hung out here a lot. Just a few questions, and I'll be out of your hair."

Desiree didn't budge, but she squinted her eyes a pinch.

"Who's the stiff?" she asked.

"Paulie Fisher, lived on the other side of town. He spent time at the tracks."

"I wouldn't know."

"Does the name sound familiar?"

"I don't like horse racing."

"But maybe you've rubbed elbows with someone who does."

"If they did, they sure as hell didn't tell me."

"I don't believe you."

"That's not my problem."

I felt a speck of blood flowing down my neck.

"He got a big check in the mail, insurance for a work accident, then died in his hotel room," I said. "Ring a bell?"

"Just because people tell me things doesn't mean I listen," Desiree said. "How big was the check?"

"Big by us bottom feeders' standards."

I heard a lot of commotion coming our way. More fans for sure. Finally, Desiree took her knife off my neck, dripping a bit with blood.

"Try anything, and you're dead."

Desiree opened the door to her dressing room and motioned for me to come inside, leaving the mob to bang on the door from the other side moments after the door closed.

Desiree Drake's dressing room was rather chaotic. Several dresses lay scattered on the floor on top of a beautiful Middle Eastern-inspired rug. Her mirror off to the side was lined with large glowing light bulbs, and in front of it were several small containers of creams, brushes, and combs. Opposite that was her changing station, a foldable wooden setup just tall enough to cover her shoulders.

Desiree put her knife back in her thigh holster and walked behind the changing station. She motioned for me to sit on the couch on the other side of the room. I moved a handful of pillows until I found some actual cushion and sat down.

"A fella was in here the other day talking about some guy with a 'P' name getting some comeuppance," Desiree said, unzipping her dress. "And then something about a large sum of money." She then glared at me as she caught me staring intently at her bare upper back. I turned away as I felt my cheeks reddening. I pretended to become very interested in the curtains beside me.

"How much more do you remember?" I asked. "What did the guy look like? Was he one of the big dogs out there?"

Desiree pursed her lips as she skimmed through some outfits beside her. "I'm not sure. He was mostly in the dark when we talked, an after-party in The Whisper's basement," she said.

"There's a basement in The Whisper?" I asked.

"If you know the right people," Desiree responded. I nodded sternly as my eyes kept wandering around her.

"So I go down there one night," she continued. "and sit in my usual booth. Then I hear some guy in the booth next to me mention your buddy Paulie, so I assume. I looked over at him, but he looked just like every other chump who hangs out down there."

I furrowed my brow and tried to think of something else to ask.

"What else can you remember? The sound of his voice? What was he wearing? Anything that made him stick out from the crowd?" Desiree's eyes wandered around the dressing room floor, as if the answer was somewhere there. Then, she shook her head.

"There wasn't anything to remember. He walked in the door, sat down at the booth next to me, took a couple swigs out of his flask, and started talking." I instantly perked up.

"A flask? What kind? Could you see the design?" She shrugged.

"Not any different from any other one I've seen. Grayish color, inlays, maybe a ruby in the center, could've been something else." I couldn't believe what I was hearing.

"A ruby? You know for sure?" I asked.

"It was too dark to see, but I just remember there was something in the middle of the flask. Why?"

I remembered a flask that looked just like that... Tony Fisher's flask. But that didn't make any sense; why would Tony want his own brother dead? Why would he *brag* about his own brother being dead? He seemed so sad and feeble. Was it all an act? I had a million questions swirling through my head, and if Desiree was right, Tony Fisher had answers to many of them. Just then, a knock on the door.

"You ready?" Bruce asked from the other side of the door.

"In a minute!" Desiree called out playfully as she came out from her changing station. Like the rest of her makeup, her golden eye shadow was nowhere to be found. She was now wearing a simple two-part dress with muted colors, her hair tied up in a bun while a scarf wrapped around her neck. The outfit was a lot less extravagant than earlier, but I could tell it still cost a pretty penny. Once again, I caught myself staring and looked away. She must have been used to people staring at her.

"If you're right about the flask, I think I have my guy," I said. "And he isn't who I thought he was."

"That's too bad," Desiree said. "You should really be careful about who you trust around here." I looked nervously at the door; the last thing I wanted was Bruce knowing I was here. Without blinking, Desiree turned to her window and nudged her head in the same direction. I nodded as I made my way across the room.

"I probably won't be seeing you around?" I asked.

She shook her head, then opened the door to meet Bruce just as I snuck out the window into the night, heading straight for Tony's apartment.

It was raining even heavier as I made my way down the street to Tony's apartment. *Time to do some recon.* The apartment building was thin enough that there were only windows in the front. I remembered there being a window in Tony's room. I climbed up the fire escape next to it and peered in. Nothing was moving that I could see, which wasn't surprising as it was the dead of night.

I was about to get closer when I saw a shadowy figure walking up to the apartment entrance. As he turned his head, the streetlight revealed his face. Sure enough, it was Tony. What was he doing out so late? I guessed I was about to find out.

Quickly, I swooped down from the fire escape and raced to the lobby. It was dead silent save for the subtle hum of a generator and would have been pitch-black were it not for a couple small overhead bulbs. There were no people, but I saw that the elevator was being used, which was my cue to take the stairs. I found the staircase and began my second climb of the night, looking for answers.

I got to Tony's floor just in time to see his door close. I knocked twice, and I could hear a muffled noise on the other end of the door. He had only been inside for a couple of seconds, so there must've been something Tony was trying to clean...or trying to hide. Safely behind his door and barely open, Tony creaked his skinny head out from the other side.

"Detective? I could almost say good morning to you." Tony said.

"My apologies, but do you have a moment? Sorry it's so late," I responded. Tony didn't move from his spot.

"Can it wait until the morning? I had a long day and am already settled in for the night."

"Are you sure you're just settled in?" I countered. "Your hair is still wet from the rain." Tony brushed his hair back with his hand, then wiped it on his chest in a bit of a panic.

"I... just took a shower, is all." His voice cracked. "We can talk more in the morning. How about Marco's?" he said as he started closing the door.

"We could do Marco's, but how about The Whisper? I hear you hang out there sometimes."

"Oh no, I told you, Paulie goes in the basement sometimes, not me."

"How do you know there's a basement to The Whisper?"

I had him there. Instantly, he started white-knuckling the door and shaking. And then, *BAM!* He slammed the door, and the chase was on.

I pushed the door open in time to see him ducking out a window. I followed him out onto the fire escape. He was climbing up, rattling the old metal stairs as he went. I began to follow him up when I heard a *BANG... BANG BANG.* Tony had brought his gun. He stopped to take some shots at me, a clear signal that he did not want me to follow.

But I kept going and reached the top of the fire escape in time to see Tony jump to the adjacent roof.

The splashes I made in the puddles on the roof were loud enough for Tony to hear, so he stopped to shoot another couple rounds. This time, I was able to anticipate it, so I quickly ducked behind the wall of a storage shed. After I stopped hearing gunshots, I ran back out but felt a pain in the side of my thigh. Sure enough, a gash just above my knee streaked red from the bullet. But I had to ignore it if I was going to catch Tony.

We jumped from rooftop after rooftop. I was keeping up with him, but I wasn't going to catch up at this pace. I could feel my body begging to slow down. I was running out of breath, and my right leg felt like it was on fire.

I chased Tony to the corner roof of the block. Once he got there, he made a beeline to the other fire escape and began to make his way down. I eventually caught up to the corner and began to make my way down as well when I saw a big pile of trash bags at the foot of the escape. It was stupid, even stupider considering my condition. But it was also maybe my last and best chance at catching up to Tony. Closing my eyes and saying a quick prayer, I jumped.

Sure, it didn't hurt like hell, but it didn't tickle either. I only wished I could've stayed in that garbage pile licking my wounds and smelling like rotten meat, but Tony was right next to me. His surprise at what I just did gave me just enough time to get up and tackle him before he could run away.

"How could you, you bastard!?" I yelled as I shook Tony. "How could you kill your own brother?!"

"No, no, no, you got the wrong idea! I didn't have anything to do with Paulie, I swear!" Tony wailed.

"Don't lie to me! I saw those bills on your desk. You needed the money and knew who had it."

"I didn't kill him. You gotta believe me!" Tony cried. "Sure we didn't get along sometimes, but he was still my brother."

"Then who did kill him? Why were you bragging about it to your buddies in The Whisper basement?"

"I was just tryna be tough, that's it! Somebody's making moves in the city, and I wanted in on it, put my name out there in case they were listening. I don't even know who got to Paulie!"

"You DON'T know?! That might be your worst lie yet."

"Nobody does! They keep everything close to the vest. But they got their fingers everywhere, even more than the Salentinos did. At this rate, they'll have all of Augustine by Christmas..."

And just as he finished his last word... *BAM!* My heart stopped, thinking he had shot me. But when I looked down, I saw a fresh bullet wound right into Tony's heart. I turned to see where the shot came from. There was a dark alley on the other side of the street and an even darker shadow running away. I was about to shake him into talking more, but Tony fell straight back to the ground as his body fell limp in my arms, dead as a doorknob.

My life never changed so drastically as it did at that moment. I held Tony's limp body in the pouring rain and bit through the pain coursing through my entire body, staring down that dark alley like my worst nightmare was quietly grinning somewhere deep inside it.

My God, I thought, *how am I going to fight this on my own?* All I did was follow a dead end and damn near broke both my legs. Against a brand new syndicate, I couldn't afford to follow dead ends. If I was going to have any chance of taking them down, it would have to be before they were up to full strength. And I was going to need some help.

I needed someone who had what I didn't: connections. Someone who could get in and out of any joint in Augustine with nothing more than a passing glance. This new syndicate must know all the big hitters in Augustine, and I needed someone who knew those same hitters.

Someone quick on the draw, smart, agile, and charismatic. Finding that person seemed like it might be even harder than taking on the new mob alone, but I had to do it.

Then I knew. If I was going to have any shot at taking down this new family before they brought Augustine back to chaos, I needed Desiree Drake to help me.

V

The next night, I went back to The Whisper again to try and meet up with her. It seemed that my luck had run out because as I was turning the corner to sneak in from the side entrance, I was met by two gentlemen who looked just like Bruce standing in front of it. I guess somebody found out about the uninvited guest the other night and guessed how they got in.

There was no way I could get in The Whisper now. If I was going to find Miss Drake, I was going to have to find her outside. In normal circumstances, I would wait for her to leave, but with two goons who could rip my arms off scoping the joint, I didn't feel safe waiting around for her to come out. I had to find another way.

The next morning, I filled Marco in. If anyone was going to know something about her or where to find her, it was him.

"You said she hangs out at The Whisper?" he asked. "She must have some money."

"Have you heard her name before or not?" I asked.

"Danny, if someone has enough money to hang out up there, they're not coming here. I've never heard that name before."

"Some help you are," I grunted.

"What do you want me to say? You're the detective. You figure it out. What do you remember about her?"

"I don't know, she was gorgeous."

"Yeah, other than that," Marco said. I thought for a moment.

"Nothing, really. Her room had a bunch of random pillows and fancy makeup...what do you want me to say? She held a knife up to me."

"Is that so? What kind of knife?" Marco asked.

"Something she could hide under her dress, how should I know? I'm not a knife expert."

"I didn't think you were, but I might know someone who is."

And just like that, another address on another receipt. I wasn't happy about trying to find someone just off a single knife, but it was the best I had, so it would have to do.

On the other side of town stood a small hunting shop. Among the things they sold were rifles, nets, fishing rods, and knives. I was met as I walked in by a guy with a scruffy auburn beard and tattered flannel long-sleeve. His name tag read "Steve."

I told Steve about the kind of knife I was looking for. He walked to the back of the store and, in a few minutes, came back with a rolled-up carpet. He placed it on the counter and unrolled it to reveal about a dozen different kinds of knives, everything from small daggers to clean your teeth with to massive hunks of metal you could fight a bear with.

"See anything that piques your interest?" Steve asked.

"Not really." The smaller ones didn't look anything like the one that Desiree used on me. "Is this your whole roster of knives?"

"These are the regular models. If you want something specific, I offer custom designs, too."

"So you make custom designs? How often do you make those?"

"Every once in a while. Usually, the regular models work just fine, but sometimes people want something specific."

"As it is, I am one of those people. I'm looking for someone who has a very specific knife. Do you have a paper and pen I can borrow?"

Steve opened his drawer and dug around for a bit before grabbing a notepad and a pencil. Thanks to my memory, I was able to sketch a pretty good copy of the knife I saw Desiree with. I gave the drawing to Steve.

"Well, is your friend a cop?" Steve asked without a moment of hesitation.

"What makes you ask that?" I asked.

"That's the custom knife every police officer gets. I've been making those for years."

"Well, I appreciate the analysis, but my friend isn't a cop."

"I don't know what to tell you, son. Either your friend's a cop, or she certainly knows one."

I thanked Steve for his service and left. There's no way Desiree was a cop, so my only other option was that she knew one. Thankfully, there were only about three dozen cops in all of Augustine, and I could find all of them down at the precinct.

Now, when you're a private eye, and you need the police for help, you usually only need one or two guys on your side. Back then, I had a couple cops help me with cases, so I only had to find one of them to give me a hand. I hadn't been to the station in years, but it still looked the same as the last time I left. I could smell the cigarette smoke the moment I walked in. The secretary, Phyllis, was still working there, and she remembered me.

"Goodness, Mister Reeves, it's been a while, hasn't it?" she said unenthusiastically.

"Too long, Phyllis. Mind if I pop in and say hello? I was in the neighborhood."

Phyllis looked at me like I burped in front of her, but that's how she looked at everyone. She pressed a button on her desk and unlocked the doors for me before she blocked her view with a novel.

Inside the cloud of cigarette smoke was the same valley of cubicles and offices I remembered from way back when. Along the walls were plenty of drawers bursting with manilla folders that were bursting themselves. One of the walls had a map of the city covered in pins with yarn and red marker writing. Phones were ringing, folks were yelling, doors were slamming. Some things never change.

"Got another favor to ask, detective?" a gruff voice said.

The good news was I knew this officer. The bad news was he didn't like me too much. Officer Greg Hobbs was one of the most seasoned veterans on the force. While most officers were indifferent about giving info to private eyes, Hobbes had a problem with it. He saw private eyes as people who expected cops to give over everything they needed whenever they wanted.

"I was beginning to think I'd never see you again. I was looking forward to it," Greg said as he inhaled half a cigarette with one draw.

"I know, Greg," I said. "I won't be here long, I just need to find someone who knows someone I'm looking for."

"I'm sorry, did I hear that correctly? You wanna interrogate one of *us* now? That's rich. Hope the case doesn't get too hard. We all know what happens when you can't take it anymore."

"One of your officers was being too loose with their knives. I haven't been here in a while, so where's Officer Drake? Married to a Desiree Drake, maybe?"

"There ain't nobody here under 'Drake', Reeves. You must've got your source wrong," Hobbs barked as he corralled me to the door I came in from. I wasn't gonna be spooked that easily, so I maneuvered myself out of his way.

"It can't be nobody! No way one of your boys knows or is married to a black-haired lounge singer and doesn't talk about it."

"A lounge singer? Marco must've been telling stories again. Now get lost before I make you." Hobbs motioned to a couple of his bone-headed friends to corner me from behind. Now, I wasn't looking for a fight, but I had to know why Desiree had a cop knife.

As I was backing away from Hobbs, I knocked against a desk nearby, sending a stack of papers to the floor.

"Hey! Can you watch where you're..." a familiar voice said.

As I turned to see the papers fall to the floor, I looked up and realized why it sounded so familiar, and my face went pale from pure shock. Even hiding behind a thick pair of glasses, a full police uniform, and no makeup, I knew without a shred of doubt it was Desiree Drake. From the look on her face, I could tell she was as shocked as I was. She looked around as if to see if a way out of this situation could be found somewhere in a file cabinet.

"Uh oh, fellas, I think Meyers has a crush on him," Hobbs said, referring to Drake. His friends laughed as Desiree's face flushed a bright red.

"Get off my back, Hobbs!" Drake said back.

"Yeah, like you could do anything about it," Hobbs snarked.

"What the hell is going on out here!?" Just then, a tall older man with a thick mustache stormed out from an office.

"S-sorry, Captain," Hobbs muttered, then pointed to me. "Shamus over here rolled in and kept bugging us, asking us if we knew some lounge singer with a knife."

"I don't give a rat's ass who he is! He's keeping you all from working, so I want him out of here," the captain said. Suddenly, the floor and ceiling were really interesting to look at to everyone within earshot.

"You're gonna talk to me in my office in half an hour about your recent behavior," the captain said to Hobbs, and then he turned to me. "As for you, I want you out of this precinct, RIGHT NOW."

I stood still for a moment, still confused out of my mind, wondering why a lounge singer had a police uniform in the middle of a precinct, but I eventually did as he told me, looking over my shoulder at Drake as I left.

"Meyers, clean up this mess before you make yourself look stupid a second time," the captain said before I walked out the front door, hearing the echo of laughter at Drake's expense.

I stepped outside more confused and with more questions than ever. I had to find a way back into the precinct without the captain noticing, but that problem was solved on its own. From the side of the building, I could hear a door open, and then out from that door came Drake. She looked around outside before spotting me.

"Stay right there," she said before promptly closing the door.

And so I waited, trying my best to process everything that just happened, wondering what the hell a beautiful lounge singer was doing sitting at a desk being treated like an intern. I didn't want to risk going anywhere, and all the captain said was he wanted me out of the office, so I followed the law, sat in the alley way, and waited for "Meyers" to come out again.

As the October sun fell and night started to come out, Desiree popped out of the door and stared at me while I sat between two trash cans. I quickly stood myself up and stared back at her. For a moment, neither of us said anything. It was Desiree Drake, all right; despite only seeing her once, I was pretty sure I could pick out those piercing green eyes anywhere. I could also make out a knife she had holstered to her side.

"You weren't supposed to find me here," Desiree finally said.

"I feel the same way, Miss... Drake?" I said back.

"Meyers. It's Meyers," she said while I paused to think to myself.

"So they don't know..." I began.

"Even if they wanted to or cared to, they shouldn't. For my sake and theirs," Meyers said sternly. I responded with a nod, at which point she loosened her muscles a bit and stood more comfortably. "I guess the fact you're here looking for me means you didn't get your guy," she continued.

I told her about the last day or so since I saw her and a new syndicate seemingly making a run for the whole city.

"With your... side gig, you can help me get tips about their whereabouts, and we can stop them before Augustine becomes a war zone again," I said. "You're a cop. You could help me if things get too hairy. You must know your way around a gun. You certainly do with a knife." I thought about the man down the alley. "I think they keep tabs on anyone they find suspicious, like spies."

"Spies," Meyers said, nodding matter of factly. "Okay, so let's review. You're asking me, a person you clearly don't know as well as you thought, to help you get some dirt on a syndicate and their entourage of spies that have magically sprung up. Oh, and you know all of this because *another* person you can't trust told you so. Did I get that right?"

I tried to think of a snappy response, but I was drawing a blank. Everything she was saying made perfect sense. She was right to think it was wild any of this was really happening. If I was any other person, I would've given up right then and there. Then again, I'm not any other person.

"I saw what I saw, I might not know you, but that goes both ways. My gut has a better track record than you know." Meyers blew a sigh of frustration.

"You're lucky to be alive, you know that? Your buddy Tony was leading you to a dead end by sending you to The Whisper, hoping someone like me or Bruce really *would* drop your body down a river." I found myself once again in a staring contest with her.

"I won't let Augustine go back to what it used to be," I said. "If I don't do something, there will be plenty of bodies at the bottom of that river."

With a frustrated sigh, Meyers looked around the alley in silence before moving her eyes back onto me.

"Fine. Go down your rabbit hole. You'll either wind up with nothing or dead. Regardless, you're doing it alone." Meyers walked back inside and slammed the door behind her.

I walked away and headed back home, in a mood where not even one of Marco's turkey clubs could cheer me up.

It was close to midnight by the time I caught the bus back to my apartment. I made my way up the stairs to my room. When I opened the door, Midnight came to rub up the side of my ankle. *She is just about the only thing I can rely on these days,* I thought. I stared out my apartment window in a daze as I thought about the last few days. I still had a lot of back pain from my encounter with Tony, not to mention the gash across my leg from Tony's gun. I had to have been running on only a couple hours of sleep, though I might have been hallucinating even that. *When was the last time I even laid down?*

I started to take my jacket off when I heard footsteps in the hall. I didn't think anything of it until I heard them stop outside my door. After a quick pause, I saw something slip under my door as the footsteps drifted away.

I opened my door to find nobody outside. I looked down and found a small white card on which the words "BUS STOP PHONE" were printed in very small, faint letters. It took me a moment, but then I remembered there was a small bus stop outside my apartment with a payphone next to it. Was I supposed to meet someone there and give them a call? Who was I supposed to call? Who was this note even from?

I grabbed my pistol from the nightstand drawer and headed out.

I was the only person there when I arrived at the bus stop. The only source of light was from inside the payphone, a single light bulb that shed a faint glow upon the bench next to it.

I scanned every inch of the payphone for notes or clues as to what I should do next, to no avail. I stared at the phone itself for a moment, then took the phone off its holder. As I held it up to my ear, I heard a voice outside start to speak.

"You're right about a new syndicate," Meyers said. At the corner of my eye, I could barely make out Meyers's jet-black hair hiding under a trench coat and fedora sitting on the edge of the bench, staring out across the street. I kept the phone handle close to my face as I turned away.

"All the evidence is circumstantial, but there's plenty of it, too much to ignore," Meyers continued. "It was risky to talk about it at the precinct. I think your friend from the alley could've been watching."

"So you do believe..." I began.

"No one will admit it, but there are cases of missing people all over the city, and everyone we ask about it is keeping their mouths exceptionally closed." I could see the headlights of a bus turn onto the far end of the street.

"Meet me at the corner of Fifteenth and Jefferson at nine tomorrow night. Bring the nicest suit you have and clean yourself up."

"Fifteenth and Jefferson. 9 p.m."

"I'll fill you in on details tomorrow. For now, see you down the rabbit hole."

The bus slowed to a stop right next to the bench. Without making eye contact, Meyers stood up and got on the bus to become its only passenger. As the bus left, I put the phone back on the hook and walked back to my apartment.

VI

The next day, I slept until 5 p.m. Guess I needed it. I got out of bed and followed Meyers's instructions to "clean up." I shaved off my five o'clock shadow, showered and washed my hair, and dug my nicest suit out of my closet, a dark blue blazer and matching tie. It wasn't a million bucks, but it was all I had.

The corner of Fifteenth and Jefferson is a ways from the center of town, an area mostly populated by a handful of small convenience stores and cheap housing. It was essentially the part of the city no one really knows about, which is probably why Meyers asked me to meet the car there. As the sky darkened and the stars and streetlights began to glow, a long limo pulled up from down the street to meet me. The limo was so clean I could see my reflection in it. It had gold accents strewn out the sides, a surefire sign Meyers's friends in The Whisper had a hand in this thing.

The car stopped by my feet, and the door opened to reveal Meyers in her full Desiree Drake getup, sitting alone behind the driver. She was decked out in a sleeveless dark green dress covered in a thin black striped pattern, with gaudy emeralds that hung from her ears beneath her hair that was tossed around her left shoulder.

She eyed me up and down but didn't really change her expression as she did.

"It'll do... I guess." Meyers sighed. She motioned to me to get in. I sat next to her on the passenger side and marveled at the limo's soft red velvet carpet and smooth black leather seats. Like The Whisper, it was just about the nicest thing I'd ever been in.

"Is this how you usually get around town?" I asked.

"Sometimes, when I have somewhere nice to be," Meyers responded.

"What kind of nice places are we talking?" I asked.

"Tonight, it's the Ivory Ring. There's a middleweight title fight we'll be watching."

"I see."

"Like your buddy said, no one knows a lot about the spies or where they came from, just that they're around. If anyone knows anything more about them, it's Sugar Allen. He's one of my contacts if I need a lead. He knows a bit about everything and everyone, legal or otherwise," Meyers said.

"Why haven't you asked him about this before?"

"He doesn't like people in his circle who ask too many questions about certain things. I can't risk leaving his circle, but you have nothing to lose."

"So what, he's just gonna spill the beans about the new syndicate just cause I ask him nicely?"

"He likes bragging about himself and what he knows. If you butter him up enough, and he likes you enough, maybe he'll give us that lead."

"And if I can't and he doesn't?"

"Then hope he doesn't pick you out and take you swimming later."

We finally got to the Ivory Ring, one of the biggest and most well-known arenas on the East Coast. It hosts a variety of shows, concerts, and sporting events, but it's primarily known as a boxing arena. The Ivory hosted plenty of big-name fights over the years, some of which you could maybe get a couple nosebleed seats for, others you'd need to pay your right kidney just to get on the waiting list.

We stopped along the main entrance, and the door was opened for us. Meyers got out first, and she was mobbed by photographers and people trying to get closer to her, and security tried to keep all those people away. Once I got out, I didn't exactly get the same treatment, but that was when I realized why Meyers wasn't worried about me getting in: everyone next to her practically disappeared. They could slip by with hardly a passing glance. I was invisible.

Meyers had clearly been here before. Another suit approached her, and they started talking it up. Meyers laughed at practically everything he said, and he led me and Meyers up some private stairs to where we would watch the fight. I assumed Sugar Allen would be meeting us there.

We found our place along one of the top balconies, a cozy VIP lounge. The couches and chairs were studded with white leather, seated around elegant white metallic tables, complete with various fruits and flowers accentuating the tables' centers. The diamond-patterned black and ruby red painted walls were adorned with artifacts and relics from past events tucked away behind a thick sheet of glass. There were a pair of dirty torn-up gloves, trophies, and medals of different sizes, as well as an enlarged signed photo of some scarred-up fellow who got a lucky shot in.

Everyone there was dressed in tuxedos or dresses almost as nice as Meyers's, making me, in my dark blue blazer, look homeless by comparison. Fortunately, nobody seemed to notice. Meyers was the big celebrity and my own personal camouflage. I essentially had no more presence than the plants in the corner.

As we walked, Meyers was greeted by a handful of people. She greeted them and made small talk. I tried to listen in, but I couldn't really hear anything.

Then, Meyers tapped the front of my shin with the edge of her heel and motioned with her eyes to the other entrance in the balcony room. The doors were opened by a shorter gentleman with a thin combover, big ears, and well-defined wrinkles that wrapped around his eyes and cheeks. He wore a British racing green suit jacket over a salmon pink button-down shirt, opened low enough to show a clump of his snow-white chest hair and gold chain. On each side of him was a woman at least half a foot taller than him. He saw Meyers from across the room and darted over.

"Desiree, sweetie!" the man exclaimed.

"Sugar! So nice to see you again," Meyers exclaimed back. Meyers bent down a bit to give him a kiss on the cheek as Sugar did the same.

"How have the shows been going? Did you talk to those producers I sent to you?"

"I sure did, Sugar. I just don't know if I'm ready for all that. What if they don't like me?" Sugar shook his head and leaned into her.

"Darlin,' if you can't sell a million records overnight, I'll buy every copy myself and throw 'em in people's windows." Meyers laughed heartily.

"Thanks, honey, you're the sweetest as always."

"Hey, they don't call me Sugar for nothin,'" Sugar said. "Speaking of the big time, did you hear about my new kid? He's on the undercard tonight! Vincent Mackey."

"Sugar, that's so exciting!" Desiree said with a hint of insincerity. "Is he gonna win?"

"I sure hope not!" Sugar laughed as he sprayed spit that Meyers expertly dodged. "He's just a steppin' stone 'til I get someone better. I get a good haul if he goes down in the second round. His opponent got ten pounds on him, so I think I'm getting a new car tomorrow, if you know what I mean!" Sugar cartoonishly nudged Meyers's arm as she laughed with him and his two female pals.

"Oh, Sugar, you're always making a deal!" Meyers said.

It was almost kind of off-putting, the way she was talking to Sugar. The calculating stare she would give me and the precise tone in her voice was gone. Instead, she spoke in a casually playful, naive manner, like everything was new and exciting to her. I recognized that look from earlier when we first got to the arena. This must be who "Desiree Drake" really was, while before, all I knew was Louise Meyers.

After Sugar was done nudging Meyers, he finally discovered me standing next to her and uncomfortably locked eyes with me.

"You lose a bus cart, buddy?" Sugar asked me. Meyers chuckled and put her arms around him.

"Don't be silly, honey. This is my... new assistant. He helps keep track of my schedule and finances. You know how hard it is for me to read all those contracts."

"New assistant, huh?" Sugar said, then he reached his arm out to me. "Sugar Allen, pleased to meet ya."

"The pleasure is all mine," I said as I shook his hand. "Miss Drake has told me so much about you."

"It's the craziest coincidence, Sugar," Meyers began. "But my assistant's favorite drink is a Bloody Mary. Can you believe that?!" Sugar looked up and beamed.

"No kidding! That's my favorite drink, too," Sugar said. "Hey, how about one on me, a little welcome gift."

"That sounds wonderful, baby. He'll follow you right to the bar, and you and I will talk later," Meyers said flirtatiously.

I followed Sugar to the bar and sat down with him.

"Hey there, Lou. Get me two of the usual. One for me and one for the new kid." Sugar slapped me across the back a little aggressively. The bartender quickly put together two Bloody Marys and passed them to us. For the record, I hate Bloody Marys. With each sip, it took quite a bit of effort not to shudder.

"Nothing better than a Bloody Mary. Now I can tell my wife I eat plenty of vegetables, you know what I'm saying?" Sugar laughed heartily again.

"You know it." I chuckled, trying as hard as I could not to spit the concoction back out.

"So, Sugar, are you just a boxing trainer?" I asked.

"Just a boxing trainer!? Kid, I do more around this city than you can imagine. Me and my people, we know everybody and what everybody's doing."

"Really? That can't be everybody. Surely there's some stuff you miss out on." I said back.

"Trust me, kid. You have no idea what I know."

"Well, if that's the case, then... oh, forget it."

"No, come on, what is it?"

"It's just... I'm a bit worried at night. I've heard... stories of people... disappearing into the night. And I just don't want to end up like them," I said, playing as scared and naive as I could. Sugar sighed and patted my back.

"It's okay, pal. Nothing bad gonna happen to you." Sugar turned to face me and pointed at my chest. "Here's how things work around here: You say nice things to the right people, you don't get in nobody's way, and you let us big fellows do what we do best. That sound all right to you?"

"I...I think so. That sounds fair," I said meekly.

"Good boy. I knew I liked you."

"But does that mean people are disappearing at night? Are they bad people?"

"Maybe they are, maybe they aren't. But that ain't something you gotta be worried about. You get it?"

"But it's just that..." Sugar leaned into me.

"Son, I think you're starting to get in my way. You don't want to be in my way, do you?" I shook my head slowly.

"Good boy." As he took another swig from his Bloody Mary, Lou the bartender slid toward us.

"Mister Allen," he said. "There's someone outside who would like to speak to you." I turned to see a guy peeking out from the doors. He couldn't have been much older than me. Judging from his athletic build and the way he was dressed, I figured this was Sugar's fighter.

"One moment, if you don't mind," Sugar muttered. He angrily got up and walked to the entrance. With all the talking around me, I couldn't quite hear what they were saying, but I could see they were in an argument. They were both making aggressive hand motions to each other, and I could tell they were raising their voices.

Figuring I wasn't making any progress talking to Sugar the way I was, I got closer to them until I was on the other side of the door.

"...you said Petrov was all set to go!" Mackey said.

"He was, but then he caught a cold, so now you're fighting Cooper," Sugar said.

"He's gonna kill me, boss! When am I gonna get a good matchup?"

"You do not talk to me like that!" Sugar yelled back. "This is a good matchup, and it's also a favor from you to me. You keep doin' these; maybe I'll be nicer to you down the line. Now, get back down there. You're up in fifteen minutes!"

"I ain't going out there, boss," Mackey said back.

"The hell you ain't. I'm not asking again. I got too much dough riding on you not backin' out."

"I said..." Mackey began. As Mackey and Sugar were arguing, I got an idea. A very, very, very stupid idea. But one that just might work. So, once again, I went with my gut and got in the middle of the two.

"What the hell is going on here?" I asked.

"This don't concern you, get lost," Sugar barked.

"Is there gonna be a fight in a couple minutes or not?" I said.

"Well, apparently not, because paper tiger over here don't wanna get hurt."

"If you had a fighter, would you get your money's worth?" I asked.

"Kid, there's no fighter anywhere. I'm cooked."

"Put me in. I'll fight for you," I said. Even Mackey was taken aback by what I just said.

"You? A fighter? You're insane. Get out of here. I'm not asking again," Sugar said.

"I'm dead serious. If he doesn't want to fight, what difference does it make if he goes or someone else?"

"I can't just bring anyone out there. You even been in a fight before?" Sugar asked.

"I was an amateur fighter for six years before I quit."

"Six years?"

"Six."

I was never an amateur fighter. And I could tell by the way Sugar was looking at me that he knew that, too. But at the same time, that's what kept him interested.

"How much do you weigh?"

"One fifty-one." Sugar looked back at the kid, and then back at me, and sighed.

"Fine. The cut goes seventy/thirty. Now get down there."

"That's not quite what I had in mind."

"Now you listen here..." Sugar began.

"No, you listen. You got a nice bet going if I go down in the second round? What about if you have me winning and I do?"

"If a nobody like you beat the undercard? I could buy the arena."

"Then that's the deal. Tell your bookie to change your bet. Bet everything on the house I win. And when I do win, you tell me what I want to know."

"Who the hell are you? You ain't no personal assistant."

"I'm just a guy trying to get some answers."

"And what will happen when you get clobbered out there?"

"Then you do to me what you do to every other small fry who can't pay you back." Sugar rapidly tapped his foot, looked at his watch, and stared lasers into my eyes.

"The locker room is down those stairs, second door on your left."

Since Mackey and I were pretty much the same weight, I was able to fit into his boxing shorts. His shoes were a bit small on me, but I managed to squeeze myself in. From inside the locker room, I could hear the rumble of the crowd much louder than the balcony. I saw a fight or two at the Ivory before, but this was different. They didn't just want to see me fight. They wanted to see me get hurt.

Soon enough, the boxing officials came in to check my vitals and my weight to make sure I was good to go. They were followed by Shay Downey, the man who ended up being my coach. He was a red-headed man in his late fifties wearing a polo shirt a couple sizes too big for him.

"Sugar told me all about the situation," he said to me. "What did he tell you about the other guy?"

"Mister Ten Pounds Heavier? Not much."

"He's an undercard, but Barry Cooper's no joke. He's slow, but he'll lay you out if he catches you. Stay on your toes and wait for an opening," Downey told me. I nodded as he laced up my gloves and my shoes.

I was almost blinded by the lights when I walked in. My ears were practically ringing, it was so loud. As I walked out, a couple peanut shells were thrown in my direction, mixed with a glass bottle or two. Good thing my "fans" had shoddy aim.

I looked up in the stands and eventually found the balcony where Sugar and Meyers were. It was too far away to really see their faces, but I could see Sugar yelling something into Meyers's ear as he pointed in my direction. I wondered how much of a heart attack she was hiding.

Since we were the undercard, we didn't get much of an introduction. The ring man simply announced our names and led us to our corners. Downey laid out a stool for me and started massaging my shoulders to loosen them up. It gave me some time to take a look at Cooper.

Even from across the ring, I could tell he was tall. His muscles were much more defined than mine, with thick, sturdy legs and biceps, his bald head shining under the lights. He was more stocky than anything and very relaxed. He probably knew he was in for an easy knockout.

The ref called us to the center, but not before Downey got a couple quick words in. "Wait for an opening. You can take him!" he yelled. I nodded as I walked to the center.

Once we were mere inches away from each other, I got my first good look at Cooper's eyes, and it made me a bit uncomfortable. He stared at me with a stoic, unblinking, almost indifferent glare. He knew he was going to beat me but was going to give it his all anyway. We touched gloves and got started.

The only thing I knew for certain was that if I stayed flat-footed for too long, I wouldn't have any teeth left. So I spent the first few seconds floating around the ring, bouncing from foot to foot as I circled him, waiting to see if he would make a move. Eventually, I bounced a bit too close, and he made contact with a right jab to my abdomen, followed by a flurry of jabs that I could only barely block. I had to get out of there, but he didn't give me a lot of openings, so I bear-hugged him and spun around until I could latch off him and get away. Cooper didn't have any kind of bounce to his step. It was mostly like a lumber. I had to be quicker if I was to have any shot of coming out alive, much less winning.

Cooper tried to disrupt my rhythm with a blitz aiming at my head. I could see it coming, so I was able to dodge most of it and even get a couple jabs in myself. I was throwing punches as hard as I could, but he just seemed to shrug them off. And the licks he was giving me felt like a freight train crashed into my ribs. By the time the first bell rang to end the first round, I thought I was going to run out of breath. Downey brought out the chair again and treated some of my wounds.

"You're doing fine," Downey yelled into my ear. "Just keep working him."

"Any other wisdom before he knocks me out cold?"

"Just keep working him. I'm telling you, he'll let up. Just don't let him get too close." I rolled my eyes and stood back up once the second bell rang.

This time, Cooper was less patient. He immediately went into me and dug into my ribs, which hurt almost more than I could stand. I tried moving around the ring as best I could, but Cooper was with me every step of the way, and I couldn't shake him. Soon, he pushed me into the ropes and started wailing on me. If I blocked my head, Cooper went into my body, and vice versa. I could feel my rib cage with every hit as the sweat moved down to my eyes. All I could do was blindly swat away at this machine of a man making ground beef out of me.

I heard the ring of the second round's end, and immediately, Cooper got off me. Practically limping, I wiped the sweat out of my eyes and trudged back to my corner. A familiar voice welcomed me as I sat down.

"WHAT IN GOD'S NAME ARE YOU DOING?!" Meyers not so politely screamed.

"I'm sorry, ma'am. Are you allowed to be out here?" Downey asked.

"Yes, I am. Now go take a break," Meyers responded. Downey shrugged, threw his towel over his shoulder, and sat down in the front row.

"This is the only way Sugar would give me anything," I told Meyers.

"By WINNING?! You think you can BEAT that guy?! Have you even fought before?!" My lack of an answer told her everything she needed to know.

"Suppose you're not here to treat my wounds?" I asked.

"Are you even listening to me?"

"I can hear you, yeah, but it's a bit too late to turn back now, wouldn't you agree?" I yelled.

"Fifteen!" the ref called out.

"What are my options? I can't take him head-on. He'll kill me."

"He IS killing you!" Meyers yelled back. She sighed angrily while her eyes darted around the room before resting her eyes on me. She looked at me and back at Cooper. All the times she came here to see

Sugar, she must've seen plenty of fights. And she must've been paying attention at least a little.

"I can't say for sure, but I think Cooper's got a bit of a tell," Meyers said. "He's trying to hide it, but he punches opposite whatever leg he shifts with. If he shifts with his left, he'll then punch with his right."

"That's... helpful," I said.

"Also, you're being too defensive out there. Stop moving around and hit him! He's getting in on you because he knows you're not gonna do anything about it. And keep that goddamn right arm up if you know what's good for you!" Meyers pulled me up as the sound of the bell signaled the start of the third round and pushed me toward the center of the ring.

I didn't make any real movements out of the gate. I was more focused on Cooper's feet from the corner of my eyes. Getting a bit closer, I baited him with a step inside. And then I saw it: left leg shift, right-hand jab. I took the hit and then backed away. This time, I made another move inside and saw it again: right-leg shift, left-hand hook. I was able to dodge the hook and make a counter jab right into Cooper's chest, which threw him a bit off guard. Keeping my right arm up, I got to work.

Sure, his punches still felt like a ton of bricks, but now I could start trying to dish out some bricks of my own. Now, I wasn't bobbing and weaving. I slid to Cooper's right and dug up under his arm pit. He tried responding with a left jab, but I was ready for it. I turned out of the way and hit him underneath, pushing Cooper back. Moving with him, we met close to the ropes and traded punches. I'd throw a couple, he'd throw a couple. His hurt like hell, and I was praying I was doing the same. Cooper's expression wasn't changing just yet. But I was catching on to his rhythm. He was gearing up for a big sucker punch.

If it landed, I might've been out cold, but I knew it was coming. As his left foot shifted, I waited until the last possible second and moved out of the way, his hand just barely grazing the side of my cheek. With all the momentum and power I could muster, I dug my right hand as hard as I could into the space between his eyes. Cooper took it hard and went stumbling back, but I wasn't going to let him get away that easy. I followed after him, dishing out hit-by-hit. Now I was in control, moving my punches from his head, down to his body, back up to his head. I pushed him onto the ropes and laid into him as hard as I could until Cooper would go down. A couple jabs later, and just as I could feel the weight of my hands disappear, one of my right hooks sent Cooper straight to the ground. A third-round knockout.

At first, the crowd was silent, completely dumbstruck. But then a couple people started cheering, and then more people started cheering, and soon, the entire Ivory Ring was a madhouse. I could see Sugar walking in with the biggest dumb look on his face I'd ever seen. I gave him a quick stare to remind him of our agreement, and he nodded slightly. Downey came up and congratulated me as I made my way back down to the locker room.

Downey helped me out of my gloves and shorts and into my suit. I felt a bit gross and still a bit sweaty inside my nicest suit, but I was more relieved that my stupid plan actually panned out than anything. Sugar came in and motioned for Downey to leave us alone. He took a ticket out from his coat pocket and stared at it without a word before looking back up at me.

"Do you usually do stupid stuff like this?" Sugar finally asked.

"Only when I think of it," I answered back. Sugar looked to the ground, and then around the lockers, and then back at me.

"I can't tell you anything about who's making folks disappear," Sugar finally said. "My people have reports of people who shouldn't be going anywhere leaving town without a trace, but we don't know anything other than that."

"I didn't get my ribs smashed in to hear—"

"I'm not done. I don't know which one, but there's a big racket being run out of one of the buildings in Augustine. They scrape some money off the top to pay for the muscle, and it's a lot of money, too. If you can manage to get the right tax reports, something might look off."

Sugar rested his hand on my shoulder before giving it a quick squeeze and leaving me alone in the locker room. *A pretty big racket, huh*, I thought to myself.

VII

The next morning, Meyers and I took a cab all the way to Third Street, about a block away from city hall.

"A racket that big can't be that easy to hide," Meyers said along the way.

"I'll see what I can find," I said as I stepped out of the cab and wrapped my camera over my shoulder.

"I'll see what info I can scrounge up in the precinct. Meet me in that alley at midnight. Good luck," Meyers said before rolling the window up and fading into the back seat as the taxi drove away.

Once she was gone, I started to feel a bit uneasy, which soon grew into a major discomfort. Eyeing the hordes of city-goers passing me, I began to worry I was being watched. Unfortunately, my fear was warranted.

I looked around and spied a tall man in a black business suit waiting to cross at the street corner about ten yards in front of me. Something about him made me very nervous. He wasn't moving at all, just standing perfectly still on the edge of the sidewalk, as if he was putting an incredible amount of effort into ignoring me. To me, he might as well have been staring right at me, watching my every move. My hands started to get clammy, and a streak of sweat darted down the back of my neck.

Other people around him were swaying from side to side, tapping their feet. This man stood perfectly still, and my gut was having none of it. The longer the traffic light stayed green, the more nervous I got. I stared lasers in the back of his head, staring at him as much as he wasn't staring at me. As if nothing had happened, the walk signal appeared, and the man crossed without missing a beat like everyone else around him. Once he was on the other side of the street, I cautiously took a deep breath, pulled myself together, and headed into city hall.

I made my way up the steps and noticed a sign on the door that said city hall was closed on Sundays. I looked in the door window for someone inside who could help me, but I saw no one, probably because the building was closed. But when I put my weight against the door to peek in farther, it moved. Someone had left it ajar.

I quietly entered the lobby and closed the door behind me. As I did, it shut out the noise of the outside world and replaced it with the hollow echoes of the city hall after hours.

After a couple seconds, I saw a janitor drag a bucket of water across the lobby. He gave me a bit of an odd look, as if he was trying to remember whether I should be in the building or not. The janitor was on the younger side, with arm muscles so thick they were like other people's thighs. He had a nametag on his chest that read, "Frank."

"Can I help you?" he asked, surprisingly friendly.

"Forgive me," I started. "I know you're closed, but I was wondering if I could pop into the records room for just a moment to check something."

Frank looked at the office hours flier on the front of the door and then back at me as if he forgot what day of the week it was.

"Oh yeah, right. Yeah, I'm sorry, sir, I'm not supposed to let folks in after hours," he said. After a slight pause, he narrowed his gaze and then relaxed before asking, "Any chance you can make it quick?"

"I... yes, of course. In and out in no time," I said. He nodded and pointed in the direction of the records room, which was on the other side of the hall to the left of the lobby. Then he went back to mopping the floor like nothing happened.

The records room was packed with shelf after shelf stuffed with documents and papers about everything, from parks and recreation to the police department to homeowner receipts. It amazed me to think that all of this precious and private information was behind an unlocked door, secured by a kid who would let anyone in with a smile and a nod.

I went through the financial records of the establishments making the most profit and took pictures. These were mostly places like banks and hotels, including The Whisper and the Ivory. Other profitable places included smaller nightclubs, a parking garage, some supermarkets, a catering company, and a barber shop. I thought maybe I should stop there, figuring there was less likely a chance a major racket was being run out of a gas station. But even so, I didn't know what to think. How good at hiding was this syndicate? Sugar said they were making a lot of money, but I still felt the need to be thorough.

I needed more time in the records room, but it seemed as if I wasn't going to get that. Suddenly, I heard a conversation coming from the other side of the door, which got progressively louder. I could recognize the janitor's voice, but the other voice, I didn't know.

I knew I had to clean up the room so it didn't look like a crime scene. What I didn't know was how much trouble I was about to be in until I looked out the window.

Sitting parked on the side of the street was a very expensive-looking car. It was a dark red with white wall tires and white trim accentuating the curves. I didn't notice the car when I first arrived at town hall, and a car that nice parked outside a "closed" establishment meant they were coming in here... which meant trouble.

I have experience with taking pictures other people wouldn't want me to take, so I quickly swapped the film in my camera with some empty film from my trench coat, and then I ducked around the corner to hide.

Moments before I was completely hidden, the door swung open. There was Frank, trailing a stocky but well-trimmed gentleman with a thick cigar in his mouth. He had beady little eyes and a thick neck. He wore a couple of rings, but his hands were so big that the rings looked as if they weren't coming off anytime soon, if ever.

"Well, he said he'd be here the last time I saw 'em," said Frank.

"And when was that?" the man barked.

"I don't know, Mister Simmons, an hour or two ago?" Mr. Simmons let out an exhausted sigh.

"Not even the simplest of instructions! I told you, if it isn't me or someone I know, you don't let 'em in. This is why you mop floors and not something that requires anything more than a second-grade education," Mr. Simmons said. "Now go back out there and make sure some other idiot doesn't get in. Go!"

Frank bolted to the lobby. Once he was gone, Simmons shook his head and walked into the records room. I kept myself hidden around one of the aisles, away from Simmons's gaze as he slithered through the front aisles to look for anything out of the ordinary, but this is when I started to get very, very nervous.

I didn't notice it before, but the aisles were built against the side wall, meaning if I wanted to get out, I would have to walk right into Simmons's way. I was a sitting duck, and all I could do was wait until he found me. Whatever he thought I was looking for in the records room, he knew it couldn't have been good. I couldn't see exactly what he was doing, but I could hear papers being rummaged through and a consistent muttering. Simmons got closer and closer to the aisle I was hiding behind.

My only hope of getting out of the room without him noticing was to wait until he was toward the wall and try to sneak behind him. If I moved too quickly, he would hear me.

As deliberately as I could, I tiptoed toward the edge of the aisle as Simmons was making his way toward the wall. I peeked around the edge to confirm he was facing away and took a couple big steps so I was now on the other side of the aisle toward the door.

The moment I thought I was out of the woods, I saw my camera, which had my name and address on it, perched atop a pile of manilla folders. My escape was going to have to wait a moment longer.

Once again, I carefully crept back up to the aisle where my camera was and stood directly on the other side of the aisle, waiting for the right time to swipe it. The problem was Simmons was getting closer to me and the camera, which also meant my escape window was closing.

Just then, as Simmons was mere feet away from me, he took a hit from his cigar, and he started to cough. I could hear he was trying to keep it down, but soon enough, he was in a full-on coughing fit. As good a time as any, I snatched the camera and bolted out the door while Simmons could only focus on himself.

Home free? Not quite. Once I made my way back to the entrance back into the lobby, I was met by a locked door. Simmons was probably thinking ahead. Even worse, I could hear Simmons start to work his way toward me, so he must have heard me speed away. I had to take a chance and walked down the stairway closest to the lobby entrance, hoping to lose him somewhere else.

The basement was almost completely dark, but the overhead lights were shining just brightly enough for me to see where I was going. Once I got down there, I took a left, and then a right, and then another right, a left. All the while, Simmons's footsteps were echoing throughout the basement. I didn't have the time to get my bearings, so I had to just keep going.

After a minute or two of wandering, the overhead lights flickered just long enough for me to notice signs for an exit. I burst open the door and started to sprint away, feeling a sigh of relief... that was until someone pulled the back of my collar so hard it knocked me to the ground. It was Simmons, and he didn't look very happy.

"Going so soon?" Simmons asked. He was as strong as he looked because he was able to drag me into a nearby alleyway without breaking a sweat. He then sucker-punched me with all the force of a battering ram.

I could feel the adrenaline coursing through my veins, keeping me awake for just a few more moments. I tried fighting back and giving

Simmons a couple licks of my own, but it didn't seem to be doing any good. Once I got my bearings, though, I was able to dodge a couple other hits from Simmons. He was much stronger than me, but I was faster. He would throw a handful of punches, and I would dodge them and land a couple of hits on his body or his head.

But none of that was doing me much good. Simmons had me surrounded, so I couldn't escape. I knew I couldn't keep this up much longer. I had to think of something quick before Simmons really did knock me out. I thought maybe I could even beat the odds and put myself at a bit of a strength advantage.

Reaching out, I grabbed the lid of the trash can next to me, using it as a shield and as a weapon. Simmons was caught off guard by it, and I was able to move him off me for a bit. But just as I started to get the advantage, Simmons's big, meaty hands stole it right back from me. He timed my attack with the lid perfectly and took it out from my hand, then walloped me across the face with it, sending me to the ground.

Seeing stars and birds spin around me, I couldn't do anything but lie on the ground of the alley. Simmons took his chance and dug through my trench coat to grab my camera.

"Can't tell what you're going after, but it can't be good for me. I suggest you stay out of my business," Simmons said sternly, taking the film out of my camera and ripping it apart. Just as I hoped, he didn't dig deep enough in my trench coat to find the actual film. I was trying to get up from the ground but could feel myself losing consciousness. Simmons left the alley as I passed out.

VIII

When I woke up, I was in my apartment, lying on my couch, listening to the twinkling sound of birds chirping. I tried to sit up, but the pain in my abdomen wouldn't let me. Midnight trotted over to me and licked my hand so I could pet her.

"Don't get up too fast," Meyers called out before walking over to me with a cup of coffee. She laid it on the corner of the table. I was still in a bit of a daze, so it was hard to process what I was seeing.

"You got hurt pretty bad, whatever happened to you. After you didn't show up at the precinct, I was looking around city hall when I found you in that alley."

"Thank you," I said as Meyers nodded.

Wincing and grabbing my chest, I slowly sat up, then told her about Simmons and me switching film reels.

"Good thing you didn't fight Simmons at the Ivory," Meyers said, taking a sip of coffee. "You wouldn't have made it out the first round."

"Maybe we should tell Sugar we got another fighter he should take a look at," I said back as Meyers smirked a bit.

"He had quite a bit to say about my new assistant. He insisted he can't be trusted and that I should fire him," she responded.

"That's probably for the best," I said back.

"Anyway," Meyers said. "This Simmons guy sounds like he's either bankrolling the racket or, at the very least, knows who is." I nodded in agreement.

"We need to get my photos developed, and then—" I began.

"Way ahead of you," Meyers interrupted, getting up momentarily and then sitting back down and spreading a handful of negatives on the table.

"These are all the photos you took."

"Fantastic. Now we just try to see if there's anything out of the ordinary," I responded. Meyers nodded.

Some of them we could eliminate immediately, like the one-pump gas station on the edge of town. But once we narrowed out the easy ones, it became way harder than we hoped. Of course, the banks were making plenty of profit, but it didn't seem that out of the ordinary. Meyers knew for a fact that while The Whisper had some shady people in it, shady people weren't in charge of The Whisper.

A couple hours and a takeout order later, we still weren't making progress. Everything looked shady from one angle and legit from another. It would take weeks for us to learn what was happening inside every place in Augustine, not the least because there would be a legion of high-end lawyers stopping us at every corner. If I almost died trying to get this info and Sugar was right about what he said, everything we needed had to have been in the pictures I took, but we just couldn't seem to find it.

Eventually, Meyers slumped back in her seat and stared at the ceiling. Taking a break from all the numbers, her green eyes sat motionless as she let out a deep sigh. Even with her thick glasses, hair tied back in a messy ponytail, wrinkled button-down, and loosened tie, I still thought she was beautiful. In fact, it got me thinking about a question I had that never got an answer.

"So, if you were a cop this whole time, where did Desiree Drake come from? How did you end up at The Whisper?" I asked. She sat up a bit and shrugged.

"Same way as you, sort of," Meyers said. "I snuck in there one night, wanted to see what it was all about. I grabbed the nicest dress I had, took off my glasses, and let my hair down. I was just another seat at the bar until Catherine Jane got the flu. Someone heard me singing in the bathroom and figured the band had nothing to lose."

"Wow, that's... amazing," I said. Meyers sat forward with a gaze that stared out miles ahead of her.

"When I'm up there, everyone wants me. Guys wish they were with me, girls wish they *were* me. I sing a couple songs, do some twirls, and wink at a couple of the boys. And for those moments, those few moments I'm up there... I'm queen of the world."

She finished her sentence with the slightest hint of a frown. It was subtle, but I saw it clear as day. I knew where that frown came from, seeing how she had to act for Desiree Drake to be loved. Whether it was the glitz and glamour there or behind a desk as Louise Meyers, there was one thing that seemed to always be on her mind: she only made sense to the world when the world thought less of her.

Neither of us knew what to say after that, so both of our eyes wondered back to the photos and documents.

"You really helped me out at the Ivory there. You must've seen a million fights there," I commented.

"I've seen a few, yeah," Meyers said. "Hasn't everyone? That place is always packed, no matter who's fighting."

"Well, I've seen a couple fights there, but it's always hard to find... parking..." A massive lightbulb went off in my head. I zoomed in on all the photos and the addresses. I got up from the couch and went to my desk drawer, which had a map of the city, and placed it on the coffee table. As I took it out, I knew I had a lead.

"Look at all the addresses. What do you see?" I asked Meyers.

"I'm... not sure..." Meyers responded. "They all seem to be... in the center of the city."

"And what do you need to do before entering any of these places?" Meyers's eyes widen.

"You have to park your car," Meyers said.

"Every cent any of these places make, the parking garage has to make at least a fraction of it," I said.

"And with all these spots combined, the parking garage has to be making a fortune," Meyers continued.

"Then why the hell is the parking garage listed making nothing compared to all these places?"

"Let's find out," Meyers said as she got up toward the door.

Meyers and I headed out in her car and took the half-hour drive to the Tatum and Weston Parking Garage. It was the dead of night when we got there. I got out and stared up at it, almost intimidated by its size.

"Here's the plan," I said. "There's gotta be something here that can lead us back to Simmons. I'm gonna start looking from the bottom and you from the top. We'll meet halfway." Meyers nodded and walked away until she disappeared around the corner. My gut started to feel heavier... like it knew I was walking into a trap.

I opened the front door and peeked into the office. The garage wasn't a 24-hour place, and it closed about an hour ago, so I didn't expect anyone to be there. I grabbed my bobby pin and picked the lock to let myself inside.

The first thing I found was a bunch of expired tickets, a handful of keys, copies of driver's licenses, and other things like that. It was all perfectly detailed and proper, and none of it pointed to anything fishy.

Eventually, I found some documents that looked like tax records and reports stuffed into a manilla folder that was not trying to be hidden. I went through it trying to find some numbers that didn't add up, but sadly, I couldn't find anything. They were the same numbers from city hall. All that told me was I had to dig a little deeper.

Like the experienced detective that I am, I turned over and ripped through everything and anything I could find: plaques, posters, desks, drawers, and chairs, but I turned up empty.

All the while, I couldn't stop thinking about how quiet it was outside the garage. As I stared out the window, there was something very eerie about an empty street only lit by dim streetlights. There was barely a sound, so I knew there was something wrong. Even though I couldn't hear anything, I got a feeling in my gut that I wasn't alone, and I wasn't talking about Meyers.

Eventually, I got over it and finished up looking through the front office, only to conclusively say I couldn't find anything out of the ordinary. Hopefully, Meyers found something.

As I got up to meet her, I looked out one more time at the window. That's when I noticed a car barely visible down the right side of the street. It was hard to make out, but it made the back of my hair stand up. I remember looking down that alley when we walked in, and I couldn't remember that car being there at all. My feeling something wasn't right was only getting worse. I removed any evidence of me being there and dashed out of the office.

Outside, I was met by rows and rows of empty cars under the harsh light. I remembered the expensive car outside the city hall. Maybe I could find it somewhere here. It was most likely to be on the first floor where the parking was more expensive.

I scanned the row of cars, all of which looked like they cost more than my entire apartment building, but none of them looked just like the one in the picture.

As I reached the end of the row, I spotted a dark area across the garage. I went over to it and saw a garage door that I hadn't seen before when I came in. I opened it, and sure enough, parked mere feet away from me was the same car parked outside the window.

Now I had proof that someone with both a lot of money and connections to the parking garage was going into city hall after hours to manipulate financial records. It was the biggest lead I'd had in days. I was glad to have finally made some progress, but I was less excited about trying to track down my old friend Simmons.

Luckily, or unluckily, I didn't have to wait long to see him again. As I was looking at the car of honor, I heard the sound of many shoes sweeping along the concrete floor. And before I knew what hit me, the butt of a rifle hammered the back of my head, sending me to the ground. I turned to see who hit me, and my hand got crushed under the steel toe of some goon. My gaze was dizzy, but I recognized Simmons's voice. He reached into my coat pocket and grabbed my gun.

"I don't like how often we've been running into each other lately," Simmons said. "I think I might have to give an example of why you shouldn't be around me."

"Yeah, you'll have to take some time off from work, maybe a couple days," some goon said.

"Maybe you won't go back at all." Another one chuckled.

Just as I was imaging my corpse sinking to the bottom of the river, I heard a handful of gunshots. *POP POP POP*. The goons got down and hid behind the cars. As they tried to return fire, another volley came, and they had to stay down. In all the chaos, I managed to get my gun, which Simmons dropped. I looked up and saw Meyers shooting at everyone, giving me a chance to run over to her.

"There's his car, to the left," I told Meyers.

"Lucky break," Meyers responded. Then, Simmons fired a shot and started up his car.

"Get rid of them!" Simmons shouted to his goons as his car started to move. Meyers and I got a couple shots in, but we couldn't stop the car without getting ourselves killed.

"Quick, before he gets away!" Meyers yelled. Hiding behind one of the cars, she used the line of cars as cover as she made her way toward Simmons's car. I took her cue and followed her.

We were still being pelted with gunfire, and Simmons was beginning to get away. Meyers got into her car, signaling me to give her some cover. I hid behind the hood of the car, and Meyers ducked under the car door to keep from getting shot. She was able to turn on the engine despite the barrage of bullets in her direction and mine. The roar of the engine was my cue to get inside, and Meyers floored it toward Simmons, who was about a block length away. I stopped to catch my breath, and I noticed a spot of blood growing from Meyers's shoulder.

"Oh my God, are you okay?!" I yelled. As I said that, more gunfire came from Simmons's car.

"Never mind that! Just keep shooting," Meyers said, pointing to the glove compartment, which had more ammo in it. I reloaded my clip and started firing back.

Meyers and I drove after Simmons for longer than we wanted. Just as we thought we'd get close to him, he pulled away or made a sudden turn. His turns were quick and unpredictable. Meyers and I could barely keep up. I felt like we couldn't go on much longer, and Meyers apparently agreed.

"We need to cut him off somewhere," Meyers yelled. "But we don't know where he's going."

I tried to get my bearings. From the street signs, I could tell we were closer downtown on my way to my apartment. Just then, I remembered one of the alleyways nearby that opened up around the corner of the block, off Fulton Street. It was famous as a place that you didn't want to go down past a certain hour, as anyone who held you up for your money or jewelry could get away from any direction.

Unfortunately, I didn't have time to tell Meyers my plan. Simmons took a hard left on Fulton Street. I had noticed that Simmons had started to drive in a pattern: two left turns, then a right. He had one left turn to go, and I wasn't going to pass up the perfect opportunity. I grabbed the wheel away from Meyers and pulled the car into Fulton's alley. It was bumpy as all hell, but we were moving.

"What the hell are you–" Meyers screamed.

"Trust me, I think this is the cutoff!" I yelled.

Thankfully, it was late, so there was nobody in the alley. But there was no way to tell if my prediction was going to pay off. All Meyers could do was keep driving straight and pray to whatever God was looking down on us that I got the timing right.

And then, *SLAM!*

Meyers's car had crashed head-on into Simmons's car, stopping both dead in their tracks. It was a complete mess: bits and pieces of metal strung out everywhere as both car alarms rang out into the night.

It took me a while to compose myself. Meyers finally addressed her shoulder wound, taking off the tie she was wearing and wrapping it around her shoulder.

Then, Simmons stumbled out of his car in a daze. Before I could say anything, Meyers hit him upside the head with the hilt of her gun, knocking him out cold. Then we just stood there, breathing heavily and staring at each other.

"You need to stop going with your gut like that," Meyers said after a pause.

"Personally, I think it's done wonders for us so far," I replied. Meyers looked back down at Simmons. She stared at him with an intense glare, and then she looked off into the distance.

"Come on," Meyers said, grabbing Simmons by his armpits. I didn't quite know what she meant, but I grabbed his legs and helped her. We moved Simmons into a small abandoned property about half a block down the street from us. Whenever Simmons was going to wake up, he had a lot to say for himself.

XI

Eventually, Simmons did wake up. The hour or so he was out gave us plenty of time to handcuff him to a chair we found inside the building. Meyers took a flashlight out from her car and shined it in his face until he rejoined the land of the living. Once he regained consciousness, he began to shake in his chair.

"I wouldn't do that," Meyers said with her gun pinned right to Simmons's head.

"Whatever it is you want from me, you aren't getting it," Simmons grumbled.

"Let's try anyway," I said. "We got you going into city hall after hours, and evidence of manipulated documents."

Simmons laughed in his chair. "You couldn't get those names out of me if you tried. I don't squeal, and whoever I work for could dish out twice the pain any of you two could do."

"So what's the harm in letting us try?" Meyers said, kicking Simmons and the chair to its side.

"Give us some names!" Meyers barked.

"You can't scare me. I'm already dead the moment I walk out of here," Simmons said.

"You don't have to walk out of here." Meyers lifted one of Simmons's legs, took out her police knife, and stuck it into his leg. Simmons let out a muffled strain.

"Who else is in on it? What are the names of those goons?" I asked.

"None of them were in on it. It was just me."

"We're gonna take you down and everyone else in on this racket with the parking garage. We don't care how long it takes!" I said.

Simmons stopped in his tracks and looked at me like I grew a second head. He stopped talking and struggling.

"Wait... you mean..." Simmons said. "You're not one of them?"

"What? One of who?" I asked. Simmons thought to himself for a moment.

"That means you guys are trying to take it down too..." Simmons centered himself and looked both Meyers and me dead in the eyes.

"Hold on, are you trying to tell us that... that you're a mole?" I said. Simmons nodded.

"I thought I was alone, I thought no one else knew about it, anyone that could actually do anything about it, but here you are," Simmons said. "Here I was thinking they found me out..." Meyers wasn't having any of what Simmons was saying. She dug her knife into Simmons's leg and pressed her gun up to his head.

"An hour ago, you were trying to get away from us after you almost tried to kill him. We're not trusting you on any of this!"

"If you have an axe to grind with them, you can have my spot in line!" Simmons said through a lot of pain from the knife wound.

"You tried to kill me twice in two days. You don't know what it's been like trying to figure all this out." I said.

"Don't I?! Buddy, I've been closer to getting these guys than anyone in this city. You think you have a shot? Please," Simmons said. "They're everywhere and nowhere, and they'll stop at nothing to stay quiet and take out hits on anyone they have to."

"Anyone, huh? Even people like Paulie Fisher, who didn't pose a threat to anyone?" I asked.

"Yeah, even people like my wife!" Simmons barked. For a moment, the only thing you could hear was the creaking of the floors beneath us.

"Your wife?" Meyers asked. Simmons took a deep breath.

"I don't even know what she was doing with a guy like me. She could've had anyone in the world. Every guy who looked at her fell in love with her," Simmons remarked.

"We stuck it out through everything, especially when Augustine was what it used to be. She always made me feel like the end was just around the corner. But I didn't see that end as clearly as she did. I took a couple jobs I wouldn't have before, jobs that Annabelle would've never forgiven me for. She never knew just how little money we had. But then Salentino got what was coming to her, and things got a lot better. Finally, me and Annabelle, we started thinking about starting a family, buying a picket fence house, the whole thing. And that was when it happened. That was when they got me in." I noticed Meyers had taken her gun off Simmons's head.

"A message came to me in the middle of the night, not asking me, but telling me to take up some 'extra work.' I didn't know what that meant, but once I got my toes wet, they made it clear there wasn't any way out, and I or Annabelle would get it if I tried to go against them. So I stayed silent, I did my job. The more I did it, the more I thought about how much safer Annabelle was going to be, and that was the only thing that kept me going. But Annabelle wasn't happy with it. She wanted to know why we weren't moving out of Augustine and why I didn't want to start a family with her. If only she knew. She was ready for the usual lies, and then she looked at me with that look she always gave me to let me know everything was going to be okay, no matter what. And so I broke. I told her everything, all the things I did just to keep a roof over our heads. Of course, she was horrified, but why wouldn't she be? She was furious with me, but after a while, part of her could see where I was coming from. But then, she told me we were going to get out of Augustine, run away so we could have the life we always wanted. I was so caught up in the moment I almost believed her. We packed up everything we had, and in the dead of night, we left the apartment."

"But you didn't run away. You couldn't," I said.

"I never saw it from the other side. We were walking to the car, barely half a block away from the front door. I looked behind me and saw her walking with me, but when I turned back around, I heard the slightest sound of shoes scraping on concrete, I turned around, and she was gone. Completely gone. Nowhere in the alleys, her suitcase was nowhere to be found. That was my final warning from them. These bastards... can you imagine someone you love more than anything, even more than yourself, disappearing before you even have the chance to say goodbye? Before you even *know* to say goodbye? After that, I had to take down whoever was responsible for it, for everything. I had to do it... I had to. For Annabelle." After all that, I had no idea what to say. The uncomfortable silence continued.

"So while I was taking the top off the city hall records, I was recording them in my own personal records for when I could really stick it to 'em...." Simmons said.

"You have a silver bullet? Where?!" I asked urgently.

"Please, the cops won't believe it," Simmons said.

"Maybe not, but if we can get it to Mayor Church, he'll have the power to get everyone on his side, just like he did with the Salentinos," Meyers said. "Tell us where it is. We can save hundreds of more Annabelles with it. We can turn the information in and put you into witness protection."

Simmons looked her dead in the eyes with everything he had. I watched Simmons put all his energy into a single stare at these strangers, who were only moments removed from wanting him dead once he gave them what he wanted. These strangers, who went from his biggest enemies to potentially the best chance he had at finally getting out of the city. But I could tell he wasn't ready. The look on his face said everything: not yet, not now. But just then, Meyers began to speak.

"I once had a partner on the force, Mason Briggs," she began. "He was brash and aggressive as all hell, but he got results. His resolve was second to none. One day, Briggs comes up to me, talking about some suspicious stuff he's been hearing around the city; people disappearing without a trace. I, like the rest of the precinct, thought he was crazy, but I was used to him being like that, so I told him he needed to get solid evidence before doing anything. Then he told me he was looking into the lives of those who went missing. Briggs got so wrapped up in all those cases that I stopped seeing him around the precinct after a while. I didn't see him for weeks until he came running into my office as I was about to leave for the night to tell me he had some evidence, compared it to a silver bullet, but didn't know who to trust other than me. So I went to his apartment with him to see his evidence. Once we got to the building, he told me he hid all of it under the floorboards of his apartment. He opened the door and went into his room, but suddenly, the door slammed shut before I could go in with him. Once I opened the door, all I found was a hole in the floor with nothing in it. I never saw him again." Meyers looked up at both me and Simmons.

"You're not the only person who lost someone important, and you sure as hell won't be the last," Meyers said. Simmons kept staring at her, then shifted his focus to me.

"How do I know to trust either of you?" Simmons asked. Meyers looked back at me.

"Because he's probably the only person in this city you *can* trust." Simmons let that simmer for a bit.

"With all the commotion we made to get here, you can imagine they have a beat on me somehow," Simmons finally said.

"What's that supposed to mean?" I asked.

"That means we better get a move on. My apartment's a bit of a walk from here, even with the shortcuts."

X

After uncuffing Simmons, he led Meyers and me through alleyways and other people's fire escapes, getting to his apartment.

"So..." Meyers said, "what exactly are we going up against?"

"I wish I knew more," Simmons said. "They make sure you only know what you have to know, and what everyone else is up to is not on that list." Simmons continued to lead us down a zig-zaggy path in between the alleys. There were enough quick turns to require us to keep our eyes trained on Simmons so as not to get lost.

"But I do know they make sure they have eyes everywhere they have to, anywhere they think they need to. They don't have an official name, but they're pretty much everywhere, right on top of you. Because of that, some people have been calling them shadows."

Simmons guided us to the corner of a walkway but stopped us before we walked completely out of the alleys. He looked straight up at an apartment complex across the street and froze, motioning us to do the same from behind his back. A moment later, he gave us a sign to keep going.

Simmons dashed across the street into a building. I almost tripped running across the street. The entire time, I was so aware of how much noise I was making. Every little sound I made felt like a bomb exploding and a giant spotlight being shined on me. Even if Simmons told us it was safe, I didn't completely trust him just yet.

Simmons didn't turn on any lights, so we had to blindly follow him in near-complete darkness up several flights of stairs to his room.

Once we were inside, the moonlight shining in from his window revealed every cluttered, unorganized square foot of his pad. Papers and drawers scattered the chipped wooden floor. Meyers and I stood at the entrance as Simmons weaved around. He didn't seem very bothered that his place was a complete mess, but I started to panic.

"Oh my God, did they...?!" I started to say.

"Yeah, they probably knew I was hiding it somewhere; don't ask me how. But I knew this would happen! Just a moment." Meyers and I could hear Simmons throwing more papers and drawers onto the floor.

"How long is this going to take?" Meyers asked.

"Not too... I just have to... wait..." Simmons continued to dig through his place while trying to answer the question. He didn't have to be reminded that we probably don't have a lot of time, but very quickly, we discovered just how little time we had.

Meyers suddenly jabbed my elbow and motioned me to look out the window, and I could instantly see it. On the rooftop across the street, Meyers and I could see a dark figure in a trench coat holding binoculars. Then, on the building next to it, I saw a similar dark figure in a trench coat with another pair of binoculars.

"Uh... Simmons..." Meyers said nervously. "I think they're..."

"Goddammit! They took it!" That's not what either of us wanted to hear.

"What do you mean they took it!?" Meyers yelled.

"They got the drop on us. The binder must be somewhere else, maybe the docks. They might have burned it."

As the three of us were about to start arguing, Simmons froze like a deer in the headlights and stared down the hallway leading up to his bedroom.

"DUCK!" Simmons yelled. In the blink of an eye, Simmons sprinted toward Meyers and me and rugby-tackled us both as a flood of gunfire filled the room. I'd never heard so many bullets shot in my life at once. Simmons used both his hands to cover our heads.

"Get up, now," Simmons said after a couple moments, and he didn't need to tell us twice. Our heads down and crouching, we followed Simmons out of the front door of his apartment into the hallway. All the while, he was looking in every direction, like he could see the shadows through the walls.

"Wait, you said something about the docks?" Meyers asked.

"If you want dirty papers burned, the usual thing to do is to take it down the docks off Waverly Harbor and burn them in the auto parts factory."

"How do you know whether the shadows got to the documents or not?" I asked.

"I don't. But that's the only place they could've taken it if I knew they had it."

"Doesn't sound like we have much of a choice then." Meyers chimed in.

At the end of the hallway, I could see the signs for the elevator, which was what Simmons was directing us toward. Simmons broke into a sprint as he dashed to the elevator on the other side of the hall; Meyers and I trailed behind. From the windows, shadows fired plenty of rounds into the hallway, so the three of us had to stay covered for the most part.

As we neared the elevator, Simmons pressed the button for it to come up.

"Stay down. It shouldn't take long!" Simmons ordered. Meyers and I were getting ready to do as instructed before we heard the banging of steps going up a staircase from the other side of the door. So once a couple goons kicked down the staircase door, we were ready. Simmons knocked out one of them with the butt of his gun before getting pushed aside by one of the other shadows. Meyers and I shot him point blank in the heart, sending him falling face up in front of us.

"Come on!" Simmons yelled.

The shadows were coming close around the corner behind us, forcing us to take the stairs. We were about five floors up, so it was a long way to the bottom. Some of the shadows came into the staircase from that same door, but I was keeping watch behind us, and I did my best to keep them at bay. By trying to focus on rushing down, keeping my balance, and aiming behind me, I managed to keep the shadows at a distance.

Finally, we made it to the first floor. Simmons directed us to a window on the other side of the lobby that exited out near the back door. I slid the window open and climbed over, falling into a bunch of bushes in the dark. When the shadows from upstairs came down, the three of us were nowhere to be found for the first time in way too long. Simmons closed the window, and we sat nervously in the dark, listening to a large number of footsteps descend into the lobby as we took the opportunity to catch our breath.

While I appreciated even the smallest moment to breathe, my body continued to ache pretty much everywhere. My trigger hand was calloused and red all over. I looked over at Meyers, who still had her tie wrapped around her shoulder, wincing silently. Simmons didn't look that much better. I noticed the bags under his eyes; like me, he must have had plenty of trouble sleeping.

"The quickest way to the docks is through Ninth Avenue," Meyers whispered.

"Too many vantage points, we'll be sitting ducks. We have to take the alleys around Twelfth," Simmons responded.

"Twelfth will take too long," Meyers said. "The binder could be burned by now."

"We're no good if we're dead. We take Ninth," said Meyers.

"We'll take Fourteenth Street," I said. "After a couple of blocks, it's a straight shot to the harbor." There was a small silence as the two pondered over my suggestion. Meyers eventually peeked out over the window once the footsteps died down and got up to signal to us the coast was clear.

"Fine," she finally said, clutching her wrapped shoulder. "Fourteenth."

Once again, we ducked and dodged through every alley we could find. Walking on even the sidewalk for the smallest amount of time was frightening. I continued to look at Augustine in an entirely new light. There was nothing scarier in the world to me than someone with the power to be wherever they wanted to be. I knew without a shred of a doubt that, no matter how many of them there were, every shadow in the city was looking for us. Every step I made felt like it could be my last one. Maybe Simmons and Meyers were feeling the same way. It might have been the darkness, but for a couple quick reflections of the moonlight, I thought I could see tears streaking down Simmons's cheeks.

Augustine's steel factory is about a half-hour drive outside the city. It sits right next to the docks overlooking Waverly Harbor. You can see the huge smokestacks from pretty much anywhere in the city. They were grayish black when they were first installed, but after years of wear and tear, they took on a rusty, golden-brownish hue.

Usually, the factory's hours of operation were like most regular workdays, which made it especially suspicious to see lights on in the building and smoke emerging from the columns at this time of night.

Simmons guided us toward a locked-off entrance designated as an emergency exit.

"Anyone got a bobby pin?" Simmons asked.

I was about to offer mine, but Meyers pushed us both aside to examine the lock on the door. She pulled out a bobby pin out of her hair and opened the door faster than her hair could fall down.

Once inside, we followed the sounds of pressing steam and whirring cogs to the center of the factory. The three of us ducked behind a corner, and I peeked out to get the layout. I could pretty much see the entire factory floor. Several rows of conveyor belts wound around the room before converging onto a single belt leading toward a massive steel-melting furnace.

In the midst of that, I counted five shadows. They all had carts filled with papers and documents. Some of the papers were taken off the carts and put in manilla folders marked with some kind of symbol, a black dot inside of a circle, placed on the folders' tabs. The rest of the papers went on the conveyor belt. I remembered the folder I found in Paulie's apartment. He must have had something to do with them.

"We can't go out there," I whispered, "it's suicide." Meyers and Simmons nodded in agreement. Simmons unloaded the magazine from his pistol.

"We wouldn't have the firepower anyway," he said quietly.

"So what now? We don't have a lot of time to plan this out," Meyers reminded us. I could clearly see the gears turning in Simmons's head. He was getting visibly frustrated with every passing second as each one shortened the time before his silver bullet folder got tossed in the furnace. I kept looking around the room, trying to find something we could use, when I homed in on the light switch in our hallway.

"I have an idea," I said. "Follow my lead." I got up and walked to the light switch, and crouched down. Next to me was a trash can filled with soda cans and looseleaf papers. I took one of the cans out of the bin and tossed it over to Simmons, who nodded to let me know he understood my plan. Meyers took her knife out and crouched behind Simmons.

Simmons threw the empty soda can into the entryway leading to the factory floor. One of the shadows noticed the noise and walked over to investigate. Once he was fully in the hallway, I shut off the lights. I could hear Meyers and Simmons make quick work of the shadow. All the ruckus got the attention of the other four, but we were ready for them. Another shadow came in alone to investigate and was able to let out a yell before we took care of him. By then, there were only three left, and with the darkness on our side for once, they were taken care of, and we could start looking for the binder.

I started by going through all the folders that had that black circle mark. They were mostly receipts for things I didn't know, with a couple of recurring names. Some folders had names that I recognized, and some had pictures of people I could almost identify.

Then, I opened a folder that had some life insurance information on Jeremy Weaver, the kid Mrs. Weaver sent me way back when. I didn't have time to figure out why this was in their possession, but at least I had a better idea why he was never found.

"Where's Simmons?" Meyers asked. I was halfway through another stack of papers when I realized he was nowhere on the factory floor. Meyers took her gun out of her holster, and I started to do the same before Simmons casually walked back into the space carrying some rifles in his arms. He handed each of us one, which upon inspection was fully loaded, and then Simmons tossed us some packs of ammo on top of that. The rifle felt good in my hands, but I had to wonder how many innocent people's lives were taken by it. Just then, we heard the roaring sound of a ship's horn.

"New plan," Simmons said. "That was the emergency signal to alert shadows. They know we're here, which means they're on their way any second. Lots of 'em. Luckily, our friends in the hallway left these in their trunk, which should definitely help hold them off." Meyers looked around the floor and homed in on a couple exits in the corners of the factory floor.

"We should barricade these doors well, give 'em one way in, and concentrate fire," she said. Simmons nodded.

"I'll look for the binder. I know my way around this place," Simmons said. "Knowing them, the others will be here within ten minutes or so, so let's get ready now."

And we did just that. Simmons directed me toward several heavy boxes and had me help him push them along the front entrance. Outside the corner entrance, we took some barrels and made a makeshift cover where we put the packs of ammo. Looking around inside, I tried to calculate how much time we could buy Simmons and how much time he would need. There were still piles and piles of documents, seemingly strung out in random places on their way to the furnace. Even if Simmons knew the place, which he probably did, he was still looking for a needle in a haystack. Actually, it was more like a needle in a needle stack.

Suddenly, we heard the faint sound of footsteps outside. Meyers and I sprang into action and got behind our cover. Soon, the footsteps turned into banging on the other side of the room. As the banging migrated closer and closer to our corner of the room, Meyers and I tightened our grip on our rifles and prepared for the worst.

XI

The first few were caught by surprise, so we were able to take them out no problem. Once the shadows knew what we were up to, they started taking cover, too, trying to pick us off. The entrance was only big enough for a couple people to get through, so Meyers and I didn't have too much at once to worry about, but it was enough. Occasionally, I'd hear Simmons's footsteps behind me, running around trying to find the binder. Eventually, Meyers and I worked out a bit of a system; one of us would fire through our rounds, and once that gun had to be reloaded, the other one would step in and fire. That way, we had consistent gunfire ringing out.

Sometimes, we would shout out "Left!" or "Right!" to let the other know which direction to fire when their turn was up. Now, I hadn't used a rifle since Rutherford, and I hadn't had to use it in a situation like this in even longer, so I was a bit rusty. Luckily, Meyers was as good as anyone could be at it. I would look over the cover as I was reloading to see how she was doing, and she was able to get shots in with the smallest of windows. My shots were more all over the place, so I had to get luckier with my shots before the shadows took cover or started returning fire. It was not easy, but between the two of us, we were able to hold off the shadows for a bit of time.

Just when I thought we had a hold on things, I heard Meyers scream.

"AH! DAMMIT!" she wailed. I looked over, and one of the shadows was able to nick her wounded shoulder. She was bleeding out, but I couldn't do anything to help her; I had to keep holding the shadows off.

"I'm fine!" Meyers yelled to me, and she ripped off her other sleeve to bandage her shoulder. I looked around and figured it was only a matter of time before the shadows would break through the other entrance. We had to get the binder. It was the binder over everything else.

"You need to help Simmons with the search! I'll be fine," Meyers told me. She gritted her teeth while grabbing at her shoulder, then after a deep breath, she sprang from under the cover and returned fire.

I dashed to the conveyor belts to join Simmons in the search. There were plenty of looseleaf papers and empty manilla folders on the floor, a sign of which documents were already looked through. Simmons saw me and pointed to the corner of the room, which had a stack of cardboard boxes stuffed with folders twice my height, and all of them were completely unopened. It would take me hours to sift all through this stuff, and we clearly did not have that kind of time. I had to find another way to look through this. The shadows had a way of organizing all this stuff, and I just had to figure out what it was.

The first thing I noticed was the spider webs and dust at the very top of the stacks. The dust faded out of view the farther down I went, and the cleanest-looking box was the closest to the floor and the farthest to the right. If Simmons just had the binder, and the newest-looking box was the farthest to the right, that had to be the place to start. I slid over to the box and took it out. It was neatly packed and stuffed with manilla folders and looseleaf paper, all with the same signal I had seen on the floor: a black "x" crossed over a circle. Once again, I went through insurance records, driver's licenses, and court documents. It was nothing I was looking for, but the dates were lining up and very recent, letting me know I was on the right path. And that's when I found it.

The very last manilla folder in the box was wrinkled and damaged, covered in ripped edges. I opened the folder and found several lists of names with receipts from town hall comparing old numbers from the parking garage and new ones. It connected at least two dozen people to the parking garage funneling scheme and thus connected them all to the shadows. It was every bit a silver bullet as it needed to be. I screamed to Simmons while holding up the binder. His eyes widened, and he didn't need to say anything for me to know he was beyond relieved.

Our celebration, as small as it was given the circumstances, would have to wait. Because at that moment, we all heard the sound of broken metal. Simmons and I looked over at the boxes blocking the other entrance and saw them on the verge of completely falling apart. In a very short time, we would be overrun with shadows in a way that we weren't at all ready to handle but couldn't even if we were. All that work finding the binder would've been completely for nothing. God only knows the number of shadows Meyers and I had taken out, and at that, we were barely holding them off. I could see in his eyes that he knew this as well as I did, and I ran over to him in desperation. At the corner of my eye, I saw Meyers fighting off the shadows that were unbelievably still coming in droves while she angled herself so as not to put a lot of movement into her wounded shoulder. She clearly couldn't go much longer.

"How are we supposed to get out of here?!" I yelled. Simmons took a car key out of his pocket and tossed it over to me. It must've been the same car he got the rifles from. Then Simmons pointed to a ladder on the other side of the room.

"There's a fire escape on top of the roof. On the signal, grab her and run to the car. Don't look back," Simmons said.

I nodded and pocketed the keys, then ran over to Meyers in cover and grabbed her unwounded arm just before the lights went out, leaving the factory floor pitch-black.

"Duck!" I yelled at her. Dragged along, she complied as she followed me up the ladder, down the fire escape, and outside to the shadows' car, just as Simmons said. I threw the binder in the back seat, turned on the engine, and backed out as fast as I could. Meyers and I were well past the factory when I realized why Simmons said not to look back. I had a sudden moment of panic in the front seat, but Meyers rested her hand on my shoulder.

"Don't," she said calmly. "He knew this would happen. They wanted him the most."

And that's when I knew she was right. At some point, whether it was when Simmons agreed to work with us, or the time in his room, or right then and there in the furnace, by the time all of this was over, he knew he was going to die. It was beyond crossing the shadows, building a silver bullet against them, and he knew there was no going back from that.

I kept thinking about Simmons and how he took these two people he had only just started to trust. He trusted them with the most important folder of documents you could imagine, his entire life's mission. I didn't think it was safe to go back to my apartment, but Meyers already had an alibi. I dropped her off at The Whisper, then drove out to the edge of town to a ratty motel just before the highway, got a room, and slept longer than I had slept in weeks.

XII

I slept so long that by the time I woke up the next morning, it was already late afternoon. Unfazed, I went over to the mayor's office and didn't wait to ask for permission to speak with him before barging into his office. He seemed to be just leaving his office, but I didn't care one bit. I dropped the binder on his desk and retold him the last few days of my life and what had happened to get it here.

Mayor Church looked almost exactly as he had in all his ads, his muscular and tall frame with bags under his dark blue eyes. He had a bit of a five o'clock shadow going on, but it almost made him look more professional and almost like a model. He was aggressively handsome, but the intense look in his eyes made him look a bit scary sometimes. Church looked amazed the entire time as he ruffled through the binder's contents. After listening to what I had to say and sifting through the binder a bit more, he closed it and looked at me.

"Mister Reeves, this is beyond incredible," Mayor Church said. "You have truly done this city a service. I will hand this over to the authorities at once, and then I'll make you a hero."

"I didn't do it alone, sir," I responded.

"I know," Mayor Church said.

There truly aren't any words to describe the rush of emotions I felt knowing I finally had done it. In due time, Augustine would know the invisible enemy would no longer have control over it. Mayor Church started describing the press conference I'd get. He even suggested a parade for me. It was beyond anything I could've ever imagined. I was so relieved I didn't know what to say. Mayor Church chuckled over my speechlessness and reached out his hand for me to shake it, which I did.

"Again, thank you for everything, Mister Reeves." The binder in safe hands, and my happy ending sealed, I walked out of his office feeling genuinely optimistic for the first time in I don't even know how long.

Just as I was about to leave the office, I remembered I wanted to ask him about the time for the press conference, so I made my way back there. Once I got inside, I began to speak when I noticed another binder on his desk that he was looking at.

"What's that you're looking at?" I inquired.

"Oh, this? Just some contracts I have to look through and approve. Boring government stuff." Church chuckled. The closer I looked at it, the more worried I became. At the binder's tab was a distinctive symbol, a black dot inside of a circle. Just like the ones I saw on the factory floor.

"That looks just like..." I started to say, and that's when it all started to make sense. Too much sense. Whoever was funneling money from the parking garage to the shadows for muscle had to have deep pockets, someone with enough know-how and connections to make it all work without drawing too much attention. Someone with a certain amount of leadership and know-how to move all the pieces around and organize a seemingly infinite number of silent soldiers. Someone who knew how to control a city.

Church knew exactly what I was getting at before I said it.

"You really are too good at your job," Church said in a way that implied he was impressed with me despite being disappointed at the same time. Once again, I was at a loss for words.

"You... you're the... it was you..." I tried to say. Church only smiled dryly.

"I'm only going to tell you this because I know you're a good person trying to help. I know this because I'm trying to do the same. And I think I have," Church said as he got out of his chair to pace around his office, shifting his gaze between me and the window view he has of the city skyline with his hands held behind his back.

"I'll start at the beginning," Church said calmly. "You must remember how Augustine used to be, crime around every corner, every alley. I tried locking up as many crooks and mobsters and dirty cops as I could, but there was always another one around the corner. The law made it impossible to prosecute anyone by the book as efficiently as needed to make any real kind of change. And that's when I stumbled on the Salentinos putting money into a new parking garage. I was at my wit's end, and it was easy negotiating with people who only want money and free rein to break any bones they like. All it took was a fake sting to put a couple figureheads in jail, and the Salentinos were in the palm of my hand, not to mention all the new recruits."

Church stopped pacing halfway down his office and stared right at me.

"Was it orthodox? Not at all. I have sleepless nights just like you, plenty of them. But whether you agree with me or not, I have done what I finally wanted since I got elected: I made Augustine a utopia. Families can walk outside past sunset, and businesses can stay open, free from the mob breathing down their necks. In just a few short months, I turned Augustine into the safest city in the world."

"You're a monster," I said.

"I prefer the term 'opportunist,'" Church said back.

"Believe me, Mister Reeves, the people in this city are free to do as they please. They are free to walk the road I paved for them however they want. They just can't step outside it." I could feel my blood pressure rising, my hands squeezing into fists.

"Step outside of it? You mean like Paulie Fisher did?" I asked. Church scoffed.

"Please. If Paulie Fisher had just whacked his idiot mob brother like he was supposed to, there wouldn't have been a problem," Church responded. My heart sank to the bottom of my stomach, and for a moment, I almost thought I was going to cry.

"I'm beginning to lose my patience with you," Church continued as he walked toward me. "You don't have to agree with any of this; you clearly won't, but you do have to be on board with it. You think you had shadows on you before? You have no idea after today. There are more of them out there than you EVER want to know. You step out of line, you move even SLIGHTLY off my road, and it'll be as if you never existed." By now, Church was right up against me. He was several inches taller than me, so he was practically looking down at me.

"We've done very good things for each other today, Mister Reeves, however you want to look at it. I'm giving you the biggest turnaround in your life, and you sniffed out a mole in my ranks." Church walked back to his desk and rested his arms on it, resuming his gaze on me. I felt sick to my stomach the way he was talking about Simmons. Turns out, all I was doing was leading him right into Church's hands.

"I didn't have to tell you all of this, I probably shouldn't have, but I did because I know you want Augustine to be as safe as I do. You might be the only good person in this entire city, and I mean that. And so, in exchange for helping me get rid of a mole, I'm giving you this one chance to walk away, no strings attached. I'll give you your press conference and your parade. You can go back to being a private eye and find all the missing people and stolen jewelry you want; I don't care. But now you know how narrow this road is, how narrow *my* road is. You know what not to cross and what will happen if you do. So do me and the rest of this city a favor, and let me keep it safe."

It was the longest few moments of my life. I thought about Paulie Fisher. I thought about Marco, knowing he'd never know what happened to his friend. I thought about all the families out there who would never know the pain of Mrs. Weaver. I thought about people like Jeremy who got in too deep with the wrong people. I thought about Meyers's partner Briggs, a good person just trying to solve the wrong case. I thought about Simmons's wife. I thought about Simmons. I thought about all those people I gave up on who needed me and how much better off they probably were now. I thought about how truly safe Augustine felt since the longest time, and I thought about Mayor Church. I looked him in the eyes and saw a man doing everything he could to keep the city as safe as it could be and succeeding. I saw a man with the same goal as I did when I first came to Augustine, and while his plan wasn't the cleanest, it worked. I saw the only man keeping Augustine from the complete chaos it seemed destined to live out. I saw a man who did what no one else had ever done, what I had always wanted to do, and saved the city of Augustine.

And that's exactly the moment when I took my gun out and shot him.

At first, I couldn't believe what I had just done. I didn't even remember the voice in my head telling me to do it. It was all a blur, an impulse made in a matter of seconds. I watched his lifeless body drop on his desk and fall to the floor with a mixture of horror and worn indifference. Maybe he really was protecting the city. Maybe he really was doing what was best for Augustine. But at that moment, I guess I didn't really care. I just wanted to know Simmons didn't die for nothing. I didn't know what else to do, and there was no one else I could turn to. I grabbed the binder, ducked out of the mayor's office, and sprinted to the police station a couple blocks away. I hastily threw a note on the secretary's desk about Meyers meeting me at Pelican Point and ran out.

Pelican Point was a beach a couple miles off the coast of the city. It being the middle of fall, there wasn't anybody there. The wind was colder than ever, whipping at my back, and I waited for what seemed like forever. But after a while, I finally saw Meyers approach me.

"None of it! None of it was real!" I began to say in a daze of hysteria. "Church had the entire city in his pocket. He was the one controlling the shadows the whole time!" I told her about what Church told me in his office and all the threats he made to me. And then I told her what I did to him. In the dark, I couldn't tell how she felt about any of it. She stayed silent the whole time.

"You and me, we're the only people who know all this. We're the only people that can do something about it." I opened the binder and started going through the pages as I walked away from Meyers.

"We can start with these names! There have to be other moles in the shadows. We can recruit them and start a resistance of our own. Bit by bit, we can take the shadows down, and then we can make Augustine a free city. We can do it for Simmons. We can do it for Briggs!" I said desperately.

Behind me, I heard a clicking sound and turned around to find Meyers aiming her pistol at me. And then I remembered what Church had told me. *"More of them out there than you ever want to know."*

"This whole time?" I asked. Meyers stayed still.

"You don't know what killing him is going to do. Why didn't you just take the deal?" she asked solemnly.

"Don't say that to me, not you," I said.

"Why can't you see how safe Augustine is? How safe Church made everything?"

"It's not real! Augustine's still a mob in control and removing anyone in their path, just like it was before." I paced back and forth, still unable to fully process everything.

"Did you not think I was going to find out eventually? That I wasn't going to know? Why did you play along this entire time?" I asked.

"You weren't supposed to survive long enough to know," Meyers said. That hit me like an anvil. It made me think of all the trouble we were in, the choices Meyers offered, and whether she was purposely leading me to trouble. I guess I got my answer on that one.

"They wanted to have you killed. You were eventually going to figure it out. But we also needed to get Simmons," Meyers said.

"You didn't..."

"And you knew how to find people..."

"How could you?! Simmons trusted us! He trusted YOU!" I yelled. "*I* trusted you!"

"I never asked you to trust me. You did that on your own," Meyers responded. I couldn't even look at her. I turned my back and dug my feet into the sand.

"What about Briggs? What about *his* case? Did you use him too?" I asked.

"Never, I would never," Meyers said. "That was before I knew... before I knew what they were doing." I couldn't believe what I was hearing.

"Do you miss him?" I asked.

"I do," Meyers said as she began to choke up.

"Do you feel bad for him?"

"Yes."

"No, you don't."

"I think about him every day."

"STOP LYING TO ME!" I screamed.

"I NEVER LIED TO YOU!" she screamed back, then paused for a moment. "I just never told you everything."

Meyers lowered her gun like she heard something and looked off into the distance. I followed her gaze and saw a large, sleek car driving toward us on the sand. It stopped in front of us as a couple shadows got out of the car and approached me. I tried fighting them off, but I was no match for four shadows at once. They pushed me to the ground, kicking and stomping on me. One of the shadows picked me up, only for another shadow to punch me back to the ground to repeat the cycle. All the while, Meyers simply stood there, looking down at the ground. Once the shadows knew I didn't have any more fight left in me, they threw me into the back seat of the car.

Before they drove away, I stared at Meyers from inside as she looked back down at me.

"They'll never care about you. None of them will," I said as the car drove away, making sure not to look back.

Some amount of time from now, I will be dead. Despite all my efforts and best intentions, my lifeless body will inevitably be tossed down some river or flung into a shallow grave, never to be heard from or seen again, completely forgotten. Nothing more than a nameless tally in the long list of the shadow's victims. Whether the shadows could live on without Church, I would never know, only that I set them on the path to finding out.

I wanted to tell myself that I made the best decision I could've made, but I didn't gain anything from lying to myself. I'd try to think of something different I could've done, but nothing I thought of ever felt better than what I ended up doing. All I could do in that car for certain was remind myself of the man who had the same car all those years ago and the lesson my father tried his best to instill in me. And with that thought came the shameful realization I didn't know what that lesson even meant anymore. It was easier to do the right thing when it came to the carjackers. Bad people doing bad things had to be stopped. Rutherford had bad people doing bad things, too; those people also had to be stopped. But what about bad people doing good things?

Church's final words echoed in my head without pause. I desperately dug through them for some sort of solace, any explanation that would grant me the peace of mind that I did anything but send Augustine down the path I feared it was already heading. But with every repetition of Church's speech, every attempt at an answer I tried, I was always left with the same conclusion. That all the time I spent searching for answers, all I had in the end was an answer I wish I'd never gotten, which left only a question I was never prepared to ask.

I spent the final moments of my life in the same car that taught me how to be who I am, watching from the rear window as Augustine shone as beautiful a skyline as I'd ever seen. I watched as it shrunk into a ray of bright lights fading into the clouds. I watched as the lights condensed into a single spec of light, just barely able to be seen. And finally, I watched that spec of light fade into the clouds and into the black of the autumn night. 95

Afterword

What the hell am I doing here? I'm a songwriter, not an author. When I write words, I expect chords to come along with it, possibly a breakdown for good measure. What am I doing writing a novel? Did someone put me up to this? Was a life of writing pop-punk riffs in between shifts at the TV station not fulfilling enough?

Okay, let me backtrack for a second. In all seriousness, it is still crazy to me that I even got to this point, a complete work of words with a beginning, middle, and end. Before this, the biggest projects I would work on were EP releases and the occasional edited video. A book just wasn't anything I ever thought of making. It was also something (if I am being honest with myself) I never thought I would finish. So, let's answer that first question: what the hell *am* I doing here? What's a songwriter doing writing a novel? More so, why is the idea of finishing one so outlandish? Well, like all good ideas, it starts with *Spider-Man*.

I had to have been in college at the latest, and I was in my room watching YouTube videos. If you look it up on YouTube, you can find old episodes from the 1960s *Spider-Man* TV show that are free to watch. It's so interesting to me to go back and look at older works of art to see the aesthetic they accidentally created; from the silent movie era to late 70s punk rock art, artists using the resources they had to make something they were never exactly able to create how they wanted. Given that, everything about the show is pure efficiency: the costume's web pattern stops at Spider-Man's torso, the body movements are stiff as can be, and nobody's mouth seems to have more than a handful of animated frames. I can only imagine the kind of show the creators and animators wanted to make if they had the time and the money. And yet, there's something beautifully aesthetically pleasing about the show in a way I don't think they intended. Something about the zoomed-in still frames of city skylines and the brassy soundtrack really stuck with me.

A couple episodes in, and just like that, it hit me: a scene popped into my head, and a list of shots, one by one like a storyboard, ran across my brain. I pictured a man running from nothing in the dead of night down a city sidewalk. I pictured him rushing into an apartment, scrambling up the stairs, and into the comfort of his apartment before, *GASP*: a shadowy man stands on the other side of his room waiting for him, his gun just poking out in the light. The next morning, I saw him dead on the floor, surrounded by police tape. It was an inadvertently chilling emotion, imagining if that scene played out like the old Spider-Man cartoons. Like all ideas I have, I let it sit for a while until I could figure out what exactly I was going to do with it, if I was going to do anything with it.

Around the same time, I read *The Grand Inquisitor* from Dostoevsky's *The Brothers Karamazov* and fell in love with it. The story follows Jesus Christ coming down from heaven, curing everyone he sees of disease, and bringing a small village to pandemonium before the titular character locks him away in jail. When Christ questions The Inquisitor on this, he says something to the effect of "People, when given the opportunity of free will, will always choose evil. Humanity must be forced into choosing good, otherwise they never will." And from that story came the idea for a story about, like The Inquisitor, a bad guy who does bad things but arguably is in the right.

Taking that idea, combining it with my idea from the *Spider-Man* show, and deciding the concept of "gangster spies" sounded awesome, so I plotted out a screenplay. I never wrote an actual screenplay, but I recently found a finished scene list of everything that would happen on my computer. At a glance, the scene list barely resembled what I ended up writing in novel form. Even so, the bones of the final novel were there from the start: a detective trying to solve what he thinks is a simple murder, only to over time get blindsided by how big the enemy he's up against is and whether he's helping people in stopping it.

Fast forward to quarantine, I was sitting in my basement with absolutely nothing interesting to do, and for some reason, I thought of the idea to turn my noir mystery into a novel. Again, I had no experience at all writing books, but it was quarantine, so what else was I going to do?

Writing screenplays was intimidating to me because there were so many formatting things I felt like I had to know and knew I didn't. Writing books, on the other hand, was just paragraphs to me. If I had an idea for a sentence, I just wrote the sentence. If I didn't like what I wrote, I just deleted it and wrote something else. The process of thinking of something and then creating it had such a quick turnaround. It wasn't like any other creative process I knew before.

Even if I was off to a solid start when I first started writing, part of me guessed it wouldn't last. I can't tell you the number of ideas and projects that were either half done or a quarter done, or not even started at all that I had swirling around my head until they disappeared from my memory. While I was working on *Shadows*, I started to get ideas for other projects like I always do. But instead of starting those projects as far as that knee-jerk spark of inspiration would keep me, I stopped myself in my tracks and said to myself, "Oh no you're not. You're not leaving this project, not this one. For once in your life, finish a project that requires more than a jam session to throw together. Show yourself that you can do something like this, just this once." And so I listened, and I kept going.

I'd love to tell you I spent an hour every day on the novel, but it was nothing like that. In the three years it took me to write this, there were many gaps of time where I couldn't think of the next scene or the right thing for someone to say. The time between writing the interrogation with Danny and Tony and when Danny goes to The Whisper was about a year of not even opening the Google Doc. I wasn't used to writing something when I didn't have any ideas, but over time, I had to tell myself a couple things: I can't let perfect get in the way of good, that my lack of experience as a novelist was going to result in writing some things that I just didn't think *were* good, and finally that I have to believe in myself; that whatever I write *can* be good. It didn't work most of the time, but as a finished product can attest, there were just enough times when they did.

Almost all the names in *Shadows* were taken from a name generator website. There's no reason behind the name Augustine. I just thought it sounded nice. Earlier drafts had Danny's search of Paulie's apartment reveal Paulie to be a cross-dresser. Meyers was, for a very long time, a respected police captain before I thought it would be more interesting to have her as a lowly officer ignored in the precinct while idolized at The Whisper. There was going to be a former journalist friend of Danny's who shows up at Tony's house and has a heated discussion, but I removed him entirely. I did use his name for Meyers's former partner, Briggs. I changed Danny's last name from "Goodman" because I thought it was way too on the nose. The boxing scene going into the scene afterward in Danny's apartment was one of the last things I wrote. Before those scenes, I just had Danny and Meyers sit in a coffee shop, see a picture of Simmons's car, and basically say, "Let's go to city hall now." My dad was the one who thought of the parking garage racket; I went to him for ideas because I only vaguely knew what a mob actually does and had no real idea how to connect the mob with the mayor and why they'd agree to work together. The entire character and motivation of Simmons were basically improvised as I was writing. I wanted some kind of mob person to face off with Danny and get in his way, and as I was writing, he became a much more central and impactful character.

The hardest part of writing *Shadows,* by far, was trying to figure out exactly how powerful the shadows were. Many times, when trying to work out a scene, I'd stop and think to myself, "What's stopping the mob from making Danny disappear right here, right now? If they really are everywhere and know everything, why don't they see him as a threat and remove him?" That was the biggest reason why I couldn't write past some scenes. Introducing the character of Simmons and the idea of a mole that risks the shadows being revealed and needing someone very good at finding people to find him quickly was my excuse that the shadows don't just shoot Danny the first chance they get.

Despite the blocks in writing, despite the fact I'd never done anything like this before, for some miraculous reason, I kept writing. Somehow, I found the time and motivation to write, rewrite, rewrite again, scrap entirely, restart, and rewrite until I couldn't think of anything better to write, and I did that over and over again until I had a finished novel. I think about that and feel at a loss of emotion because I've spent so long associating *Shadows* with another unfinished idea I had, something I would eventually forget about and throw away with all the other incomplete projects. And yet, here we are. Writing *Shadows* has been one of the biggest challenges I've ever given myself, and finishing it has been one of my greatest joys. I can't wait for what the future brings, whether it's musical, literary, or something else completely different I decide to take on. Hopefully, the next time I take on a major project in a medium I've never done before, I won't mull over the details too much, even though I know I probably will. Nevertheless, here's to the next chapter, here's to the next project, and here's to the future.

About the Author

Gabe Straight was born and raised in Dedham, Massachusetts. He attended Emerson College and later went into the broadcasting industry. In his free time, Gabe is primarily a songwriter, having released a number of EPs and songs under different projects. He also enjoys watching football, cooking, and playing games of any kind. This is his debut literary work. He currently lives in Framingham, Massachusetts.